W9-CXL-648

She knew he wouldn't peek....

Darn it! Cassie undressed and neatly lay her clothes on a nearby rock. From behind the tarp Michael had rigged, she was aware of his every move as he set up camp. She gingerly pulled the cord of the bucket above her, and a narrow stream of warm water cascaded over her head and across her shoulders.

"Are you sure I don't have to save any for you?" she called out breathlessly. *Or make room for you?*

"No. I'm warming some for myself now. I'll shower after you're done."

What if she sneaked a peek at him? He must have a wonderful body—lean and hard, with muscular legs that go on forever. She shivered—and not from the chilled air.

The forest around her was still and hushed. Beyond their clearing in the forest, there was not another living soul.

How much longer could she take it . . . being alone with Michael Longlake?

ABOUT THE AUTHOR

Charlotte Maclay has always enjoyed the outdoors and loves nothing more than sitting in a comfortable chair under a pine tree, reading a good book. Her first trip to her husband's old stomping grounds, the boundary waters of northern Minnesota, was a wonderful adventure. She couldn't resist turning the magical vistas of pines and firs, broad expanses of crystal clear water and the mournful call of a loon into a story of romance. When not vacationing in the woods, Charlotte and her husband live in Southern California and are both actively involved in their local community.

Books by Charlotte Maclay

HARLEQUIN AMERICAN ROMANCE
474—THE VILLAIN'S LADY
488—A GHOSTLY AFFAIR
503—ELUSIVE TREASURE

CHARLOTTE MACLAY

MICHAEL'S MAGIC

Harlequin Books

TORONTO • NEW YORK • LONDON
AMSTERDAM • PARIS • SYDNEY • HAMBURG
STOCKHOLM • ATHENS • TOKYO • MILAN
MADRID • WARSAW • BUDAPEST • AUCKLAND

Dedicated to the families who live along the
Gunflint Trail

ISBN 0-373-16532-3

MICHAEL'S MAGIC

Copyright © 1994 by Charlotte Lobb.

All rights reserved. Except for use in any review, the reproduction or utilization of this work in whole or in part in any form by any electronic, mechanical or other means, now known or hereafter invented, including xerography, photocopying and recording, or in any information storage or retrieval system, is forbidden without the written permission of the publisher, Harlequin Enterprises Limited, 225 Duncan Mill Road, Don Mills, Ontario, Canada M3B 3K9.

All characters in this book have no existence outside the imagination of the author and have no relation whatsoever to anyone bearing the same name or names. They are not even distantly inspired by any individual known or unknown to the author, and all incidents are pure invention.

This edition published by arrangement with Harlequin Enterprises B. V.

® and TM are trademarks of the publisher. Trademarks indicated with ® are registered in the United States Patent and Trademark Office, the Canadian Trade Marks Office and in other countries.

Printed in U.S.A.

Chapter One

With a silent dip of the paddle, the canoe surged smoothly through the bronzed reflection of the setting sun. Nearby, a loon flapped its black wings in a territorial display, then lifted itself off the wide expanse of water that separated Canada from northern Minnesota. As the graceful bird departed, it warbled a mournful call.

His paddle resting across the gunnels of the birchbark canoe, Michael Longlake watched the bird's effortless flight. He sensed a waiting upon the land, an anticipation along the shore and deep within the woods. He hadn't had such a feeling since he was a boy, and the sensation weighed heavily on his broad shoulders.

The evening breeze riffled the water and fluttered the ends of his long ebony hair, shifting the strands across his forehead. With a determined effort, he set aside thoughts of his youth and slid the paddle into the water again, stroking toward home. The pines and firs along the shore were a dark green in the fading light. Only the glow from the small building that housed Boundary Water Canoes, Inc., shone through the trees.

Minutes later he feathered the canoe beside a sandy beach. His boots made little splashes as he stepped agilely out of the boat and lifted it from the water.

An old man with shoulder-length gray hair walked down the gentle slope toward Michael. Even using a walking stick to compensate for his limp, the man exuded the dignity and power that was formally his by right of tribal leadership.

"Good evening, Grandfather," Michael acknowledged as he lifted a day pack from the canoe.

"Did you feel it?" Snow Cloud asked.

"Feel what?" He turned the craft over to drain the few drops of water that had settled in its bottom.

"The Dream Catchers. They are restless tonight and are making a crease in time."

Michael knew the myths of his people, but years ago he'd given up believing in them. Now he took life one day at a time, hoping his feelings of guilt would gradually subside.

"A time of testing is coming," the old man insisted when Michael didn't respond.

"I was tested and failed."

With a weary shake of his head, Snow Cloud said, "Perhaps you will be given a second chance. You must be ready."

BY THE NEXT MORNING, when Michael heard a car pull up in front of his workshop, he had forgotten his conversation with his grandfather. He didn't bother to check who the visitor might be. A customer for one of his hand-built canoes would know where to find him; anyone else wasn't worth the trouble of interrupting the careful process of molding birchbark across a frame of white cedar.

"Yoo-hoo! Anyone home?"

Michael's hands stilled. The woman's voice sounded as melodious and cheerful as a songbird in spring. "Back here," he called. "Through the double doors."

She appeared in the doorway, backlit by the morning sun. Short blond hair haloed her face. Against the glare, he noted a slender figure with a tiny waist above the feminine curve of her hips, and slim legs snugged into tight-fitting jeans.

"Hi, there. You Michael Longlake?" Light on her feet, she blew into the workshop with the energy of a small hurricane. "This place of yours sure isn't easy to find. I must have made a dozen wrong turns before I found the right road. Doesn't anyone believe in signs around here?"

She halted right next to him, the top of her head about level with his chin, and gave him the brightest smile he had ever seen. "I'm Cassie Seeger. From Minneapolis. Well, sort of. I really live in Deephaven, which is about thirty miles from the city. Out by Lake Minnetonka? You know. Like in Tonka trucks. Only they moved the factory a while ago. I don't remember where to."

Michael didn't know what had happened to the toy factory, either—nor did he care. He did know that Cassie Seeger was about the most energetic bundle of enthusiasm he had ever met. The light scent of perfume warmed by all that energy reminded him of springtime, wildflowers . . . and sex.

"Was there something you wanted, Ms. Seeger?"

"Oh, sure." She waved her hand in easy dismissal. "I know I tend to rattle on. That's because I spent so much time with Aunt Myrtle and she never let me get a word in edgewise when I was a kid, so now when I get a chance I just keep talking. But don't worry, I promise I won't get on your nerves. I know when to keep quiet, too."

"I'm glad to hear that." In spite of himself, a smile twitched the corners of Michael's lips. Spending time with Cassie would be like hanging around with a whirlwind.

"Some of the regulars who come in for breakfast at the coffee shop where I work don't like a whole lot of chatter first thing in the morning, so I serve 'em up their coffee real quietlike. In no time at all they're talkin' and carryin' on like usual and ready to go to work. It's the way they like to start their day."

"Ms. Seeger, I have the distinct impression I'm missing something."

"Like what?" she asked brightly, the blue of her eyes glistening with a mischievous spark.

"Like why you have arrived at my shop?"

"Oh, that." She hooked the back of her wrist at the curve of her hip. "Why, I want you to guide me, of course."

Guide her? As in a canoe trip?

He'd consider kissing that mobile mouth of hers, just to shut her up for a minute, and he'd even think about taking that sweet little body of hers to bed. But he had more sense than to take a trip with Cassie Seeger out into the woods all alone. This woman was a definite threat to a guy's hard-earned tranquillity!

"Sorry, Ms. Seeger. I don't do guiding anymore. I suggest you try at Canoe Country Safaris. About five miles back down the road. That's their business."

"I did try." Her cheerful expression dissolved like melting candle wax. "They were all booked."

"There are a couple of other places...."

"I've tried them all. Every last one between here and Grand Marais. You're my last hope."

"I know August is pretty busy for tourists around here, but there should be somebody available. At least you could probably plug into a group trip."

"Well, see, the real problem is where I want to go." A deep sigh raised the swell of her breasts beneath her cotton shirt, forcing Michael to clench his teeth against a heated and totally unexpected surge of desire. "Or maybe it's *what* I'm looking for."

He didn't like the sound of that. She didn't exactly look like your typical uranium hunter who showed up in the north woods. And Lord knew what other crazy scheme she might have in mind. "What are you trying to find?" He held his breath waiting for her answer.

"An enchanted village," she admitted softly.

He was dumbstruck. Her announcement pinged around in his head like a ball in a tilted pinball machine. Ignoring a niggling pain that started at the base of his skull, he rolled his eyes toward heaven. "Right."

"Now, don't say it like that. You of all people ought to be willing to believe in the stories of your ancestors."

"I don't believe in myths, Ms. Seeger, Indian or otherwise."

She stabbed him in the chest with a slender finger. "It's not a myth! Way Quah is real! And will you quit calling me *Ms.* in that condescending way. I have found references to an enchanted village in a dozen different books, and I've actually located it on a satellite map. Nobody..." She jabbed him again. "Nobody is going to tell me Way Quah is not there."

He held up his hands in mock surrender. "If that's what you want," he said, his usually calm temper rising, "your little enchanted village exists. But I'm not going to take you there or anyplace else, and that's final."

Her quivering chin gave him a gut-twisting case of the guilts, and so did the sudden pool of tears in her eyes. "All right—" her voice caught "—I'll just have to go there by myself."

She whirled away and defiantly marched toward the door.

Michael stifled a groan. "Wait a minute." He caught up with her before she reached her car, a fender-dinged compact that had seen better days. "Have you ever even been in a canoe before?"

She tried to open the driver's door, but he held it shut with the press of his palm.

"What difference does it make to you?" she asked with a haughty lift of her wobbly chin.

"None. Except I'm part of the local rescue squad. You get yourself in trouble out there, I've gotta come get you and haul your little fanny back home."

"I can take care of my own 'fanny,' thank you very much." She tugged on the door handle, to no avail. "I've been on my own since I was fifteen, *Mr.* Longlake. Eleven years. And I don't need you or anybody else to tell me what I can or cannot do."

That news made Michael reassess his opinion of the lady. Her flawless, youthful complexion made her look about eighteen, not twenty-six. He hated the thought of her fair, delicate skin getting sunburned out on the lakes. But he guessed that was her business, not his.

"Paddling a canoe isn't as easy as it looks," he warned.

"I know that. I've read all about canoeing, and wilderness trips, and camping and stuff like that at the library."

"Library?" he echoed. Worse and worse. The woman was a disaster waiting to happen. Little wonder no outfitter this side of Grand Marais would have anything to do with her.

"I go to the library every Tuesday—that's my day off—and I find the experience very informative. If you'd like, I can recommend some books for you on *tact.*"

He felt it again, that unfamiliar twitch of his lips— an urge to laugh somewhere deep in his gut. Cassie managed to have quite an effect on his sense of humor, as well as a substantial impact on his libido. "What about portaging? Do you have any idea how heavy a canoe can get after carrying it for only a quarter mile?''

"You know how much a tray filled with meals for six can weigh?" she countered. "Carried one-handed?''

"There are wild animals out there. Aren't you afraid of being attacked?''

"No more than I'm afraid of being mugged in the city. Frankly, I'd rather take my chances with an angry bear than some guy on dope.''

He had to give her points for thinking fast on her feet. But no amount of street smarts could compensate for lack of experience in the wilderness.

"Look, Ms.... Cassie," he corrected himself, lowering his voice. "It takes a lot of gear for a canoe trip. You can't possibly have everything you need—''

"I've got all my personal stuff—heavy-duty rain gear, thermal underwear, three pairs of wool socks, a water purifier...you name it, I've got it. I have a list. The rest I plan to rent. I've been saving up for nearly a year.''

He glanced into the back seat of the car at a stack of equipment. Right on top were a half-dozen boxes of Hostess Twinkies. He did a mental double take. With Cassie, dinners around the camp fire ought to be a real gourmet treat.

"This map you're talking about," he persisted. "How can you possibly spot an enchanted anything on a map?"

"I'll show you."

Before he realized what was happening, she'd ducked under his arm, pulled open the back door and was rummaging through her stack of gear. A moment later she presented him with an infrared map of the northern Minnesota-Canadian border area. She spread it out on the rust-spotted hood of the car.

"There." She indicated a minuscule point of white in a sea of artificial greens and blues showing forests and winding waterways along the border country. "See how the edges are square."

Michael knew the area. At least, he thought he did. "There's nothing out there except trees and water."

"Then tell me what kinds of trees grow in neat little squares."

He frowned. For a moment, so quick he wouldn't have admitted it to another living soul, he had a flash of his adolescent vision quest, a village he'd seen while under the influence of near starvation, dehydration and too much sun—wigwams set in a careful square bordering a ceremonial area. "Maybe it's a camp set up for back-country tourists."

"Too big."

"Then an old timber-cutting site."

"I've researched the entire area. It's virgin forest. There's never been any logging there."

He puzzled over her answers and the map. "Maybe it's an electronic glitch in the satellite photo. A mistake in printing." He knew damn well it wasn't an enchanted village, forget how he had heard the tales of such a place as a kid sitting around his grandfather's camp fire. He had long since outgrown those superstitions.

"There's only one way to be sure."

Folding up the map with the same care he kept his emotions in check, he said, "Have a nice trip."

She visibly paled. "You won't help? Even after what I've shown you?"

"No."

CASSIE'S HANDS SHOOK as she drove away from Michael Longlake's canoe shop. She double-damned him, not only for his refusal to help her find the enchanted village, but for his dark, sexy eyes.

Onyx, she recalled, a gaze so penetrating her knees had gone weak and she'd felt her heart thudding against her ribs.

Good grief! She had never reacted in quite that way to any man. And certainly hoped she never would again.

Lust, she decided. Pure and simple. At first sight, her thoughts had taken a mental leap to hot, sweaty bodies and rumpled sheets. Unusual thoughts for her, to say the least.

There was something very elemental about the man. His burnished complexion and his straight dark hair skimmed back from his forehead appealed to her in a basic way; his dark eyes had gazed at her from beneath equally raven brows. Well-defined cheekbones and a strong jawline had drawn her attention to firm, sensuous lips. *Kissable* lips, she thought, swallowing uncomfortably.

The car skidded around a corner on the narrow road and she slammed on the brakes.

Lord, she'd be better off braving the wilderness alone than being tempted by a hunk like Michael Longlake. The pervasive scent of cedar and birch in his shop still clung to her clothing, reminding her of his overwhelming presence.

A few minutes later, she turned in at the entrance to a run-down fishing lodge where she'd reserved a room for the night. She'd arrange to rent whatever she needed from the outfitters and be on her way in the morning, just as she'd planned. Nobody, not even a guy who oozed sex appeal, would stop her from pursuing her dream. After all, the folks at Arletta's Coffee Shop were counting on her to find Way Quah's secret of happiness.

MICHAEL HAD WATCHED Cassie's car roar away from his shop, wincing when she nearly took out a sapling pine at the edge of the driveway. The woman was a menace. He ought to notify the Forest Service on both sides of the border to evacuate the entire area from here to Winnipeg.

Spearing his fingers through his hair, he turned back to his workshop only to be confronted by his grandfather.

"Why did you not agree to guide the woman?" Snow Cloud asked.

"She's a nut case. She's looking for something that doesn't exist."

"Are you so sure?"

A picture of the phantom village flashed through Michael's mind again, followed by a sense of euphoria and the fleeting image of a woman he would grow to love, then lose. *His fault,* his conscience reminded him with whiplash force. "Of course I'm sure. It was only a hallucination."

"When you came home from your vision quest you were sure Way Quah was real."

"I was just a kid." Michael walked past his grandfather into the shade of the workshop. "I gave up chasing after dream images a long time ago." When his wife Monica had died, along with their child, Michael had set his youth and all of the hopes he'd once held behind him. It was better that way, he thought grimly.

Snow Cloud wasn't put off by the back Michael turned to him. "In some way, that woman who was here is connected to you. She shares your dream. I feel it is so and believe you feel it, too. That is enough reason for you to journey with her."

"I'm not going anywhere, Grandfather." Michael bent over his work, layering pine gum along a seam of the canoe for glue. He made the craft in the old way as he had learned it from his father and grandfather. Most often his customers were museums or collectors. Most people preferred more practical fiberglass construction for their canoeing adventures. For lengthy trips, so did Michael.

"If you do not go with her, she will fail," Snow Cloud warned.

"She'll fail because there's nothing magical out there to find."

"You are wrong, son of my son. The Dream Catchers will welcome you if you are willing to open your heart."

Superstitious nonsense.

As CASSIE DINGED the visitors' bell on the registration counter of Lakeside Lodge, she noted the signs of decline. The wooden floor could have used a refinishing job, posters tacked to a corkboard announcing special events were seriously outdated, and the rustic furniture arranged around a giant rock fireplace needed reupholstering. Dozing on the floor next to the counter, the resident hound dog looked to be as old and tired as the decor.

"Hi ya, fella," Cassie said, bending to give him a pat. "Looks like you've already had a hard day."

His tail flicked twice in friendly response, and he gazed up at her with milky eyes.

"'Fraid his workin' days are over," said the woman who appeared behind the counter. Her weary smile didn't quite reach her eyes. "Wish I could say the same for myself." With an aging hand twisted by arthritis, she shoved a registration slip across the counter. "You'd be wanting a room?"

"Yes, ma'am. I called for a reservation. Just one night."

"Seeger, right? We don't get many calls since we stopped advertising. Had to 'cause I couldn't keep up, what with my husband not able to get around any better than that ol' dog down there."

Cassie filled out the form with her name and address. "I'm sorry to hear about your husband, ma'am."

"We all gotta get old sometime, I suppose, but I surely do wish we could sell this place and move south. Florida, maybe. Winters are gettin' just too hard on our ol' bones." She pulled a room key from a slot behind her and passed it across the counter to Cassie. "Cabin is outside and to your right, just up from the beach. I'm Agnes Rassmusen. If you need me, just holler. Enjoy your stay."

"Yes, ma'am. And I hope you and your husband get to feeling better soon." That didn't seem like a reasonable prospect, but Cassie wanted to wish the woman well. Knowing how much effort it took to run a coffee shop, she could easily imagine the work entailed in operating a lodge with a small dining room.

As she headed toward her assigned cabin, she inhaled deeply of the scent of pine and wood smoke drifting on the air. Smiling to herself, Cassie decided if she didn't have to get back to Arletta's café, and had enough money in the bank, she might consider buying Lakeside Lodge herself.

THE TOM-TOM THAT BEGAN beating at midday right outside Michael's workshop wasn't simply nonsense. It was downright irritating.

Snow Cloud had taken up a position right next to the door. Draped with a blanket, an eagle feather stuck in his hair, the old man sat on the ground beating a steady rhythm on the taut skin drum.

Michael's nerves drew equally strained as the afternoon wore on. Stubborn old fool. He couldn't very well throw his own grandfather off his property. But he was damn well tempted.

Hours later Michael decided he'd reached his limit.

He marched out of his workshop. The headache that had started that morning with Cassie was a roaring pain that vibrated through his entire body with each beat of the drum. He'd take that crazy lady on a canoe ride she'd never forget—he'd make sure of it.

Then he'd come back home—thumb his nose at his grandfather, with all due respect—and get on with his business. Alone.

"You've won, Snow Cloud," Michael announced, folding his arms across his chest, feeling not the least amount of remorse for his decision to give Cassie Seeger a hard time. "If you can find her, have her at my house tomorrow before dawn."

The tom-tom tempo accelerated. A sly smile crossed Snow Cloud's weather-worn face.

Michael's spine reacted to the new rhythm with a disturbing shudder. He had the distinct impression he'd just agreed to a whole lot of trouble.

Chapter Two

Cassie gave a quick swipe of her palm on her jeans before she knocked at Michael Longlake's front door. In spite of the cool morning air, she was sweating. She had no idea why Michael had changed his mind about guiding her, but the old man had assured her everything would be just fine.

Snow Cloud was a sweetie pie, she decided. He reminded her a lot of Marty Rosenheimer, who showed up every morning at the coffee shop and hung around till noon just because he was lonely. Although Cassie had had plenty of second thoughts about going anywhere with Michael Longlake, she felt she couldn't disappoint his grandfather. Oddly enough, it had seemed very important to him that she and his grandson make this journey. She couldn't imagine why.

Oh, well, in for a penny, in for a pound, as her Aunt Myrtle used to say.

Cassie rapped her knuckles sharply on the varnished pinewood door. Though not large, the house looked cozy, nestled as it was among pines and firs within shouting distance of Michael's workshop. From the porch, the view of Gunflint Lake stretched into the misty distance like an Impressionist painting Cassie had once seen at the Minneapolis Museum of Art—all muted colors with everything slightly out of focus, and prettier because of it.

The door was yanked open with such force she gasped . . . which was better than uttering the heated groan that rose in her throat at the sight of Michael Longlake.

His dark hair glistened with moisture, as though he'd just stepped out of the shower. His mottled camouflage shirt hung open, revealing a broad, rock-hard chest and a solid, no-nonsense stomach. Below that, his jeans hung low on his lean hips and . . .

Cassie's gaze whipped up to meet his. She wasn't going to notice his pants were unsnapped. She wouldn't think about it. Or about the naked flesh that dipped into hiding below the waistband. She frantically studied the sensuous curve of his lips and the interesting angle of his jaw to avoid concentrating on lower parts of his anatomy, only to conclude, top to bottom, this guy would cause havoc in a nunnery.

"'Morning." The cheerful greeting hitched in her throat. She tried for a tentative smile. "Am I too early? I'll come back at noon, if you'd like. When you've had plenty of time to get dressed."

"Come on in." His baritone voice had a raspy quality, as though the words he'd spoken were his first of the day.

"Your grandfather said..." He turned away before she could finish her thought, leaving Cassie standing in the open doorway.

With a shrug, she followed him inside. Some people simply weren't scintillating conversationalists so early in the day.

He padded barefoot across the carpeted living room, then through a swinging door into the kitchen, and poured himself a cup of coffee. "Want some?" he called to her.

"No, that's okay. I got some breakfast at Lakeside Lodge where I stayed. Mrs. Rassmusen was as busy as a firefly on the Fourth of July. I lent her a hand as best I..."

Carrying the oversize mug, he crossed the living room again to another doorway and silently vanished down a hall. Good grief, the guy even had gorgeous feet! Cassie thought, blowing out a sigh. It seemed a little late in life for her to develop a foot fetish, but for the first time she could actually conceive of the possibility.

Left to her own devices, Cassie surveyed her surroundings. Compared to her small apartment over a garage, Michael's home was spacious. Country decor and cute little ceramic pieces on maple end tables hinted at a woman's touch, but the general clutter of unopened mail and a stray sock or two peeking out from under the robin's egg blue couch suggested bachelor quarters.

Then she spotted the photo on the mantel above the rock fireplace.

"It figures," she mumbled, wandering over for a closer look. "All the good ones are taken." Not that Michael appeared to be all that much fun in the morning, she conceded.

His wife was a dark-haired knockout. Their son, who looked to be about two, was equally attractive and had a smile that would someday make him a lady-killer, just like his dad.

Carefully lifting the photo from the mantel, Cassie said, "Well, shoot. Too late again, Cassandra Seeger."

"Put that down!"

Michael's bellow from across the room nearly made Cassie lose her grip on the picture. He stormed toward her, his booted feet shaking the house with each step, and pulled the photo from her hands. With the back of his sleeve, he dusted the glass in a hurried swipe and returned the silver-framed picture to its place of honor on the mantel.

"I wasn't going to damage it, for pity's sake," she said, irritation twisting one corner of her mouth. "I was just admiring your wife and son. She's beautiful. So's the boy."

"Yes." His soft reply held a definite strain, enough so Cassie gave him a confused look.

"I hope I didn't wake them by knocking so loud." Though his angry shout had likely been a lot more disturbing to anyone still trying to sleep than her rap on the door.

He gave a quick shake of his head. "Not likely. They're both dead. I killed them." With a visible effort, he pulled his gaze away from the photo and looked down at Cassie. Dark misery filled his eyes. "Let's go," he ordered.

If Cassie had been chewing gum, she would have choked on it.

Michael had *killed* his wife and child? And she was about to go out into the wilderness alone with him? Snow Cloud wouldn't send her off alone with a *murderer,* for heaven's sake . . . would he?

Michael blasted out the front door so fast she was left standing slack jawed on the porch watching him head across the yard.

He didn't stop until he reached his workshop, hefted the food pack from the oversize freezer and stuffed it into the waiting Cordura portage pack. Michael didn't like what Cassie Seeger did to him, didn't like what she made him think about—the love of a woman and the guilty sense of loss.

With that head of tousled blond curls, Cassie looked as if she had awakened only moments ago after a good night of hot sex. And that damn smile of hers. Innocent and sexy as hell all at the same time. It put his teeth on edge. Certain other parts of his anatomy had gotten restless, too, and he didn't want that. Nor did he need such cheerfulness the first thing in the morning.

His plan was to get rid of Cassie as fast as possible. That was the only way he'd get any peace of mind. He sure as hell had spent a restless night thinking about her...and this damn trip. Little wonder he'd overslept.

With what he had in mind, he figured she'd endure no more than twenty-four hours on the lakes—max. Then he could put this whole mess behind him.

Living like a near hermit was just how he preferred it.

When Michael reappeared from his workshop, Cassie found herself the recipient of several barked orders that sent her scurrying around without a moment to think, getting her gear and putting it into the boat. Instead of birchbark, as she'd half expected, this canoe had a sleek Kevlar finish with a slight flare along either side and a seat at each end.

The next thing she knew she was sitting in the bow of the canoe, paddle in hand, the camera borrowed from a friend stowed with the rest of her gear, as Michael pushed them away from shore.

She'd never had a second to object, or ask him to explain his earlier remark, though in her heart of hearts she couldn't believe that Michael could be a killer.

By now it was too late to turn back, anyway. Cassie was already caught up in the beauty of the day, the air crisp and fresh, with only a hint of the heat that was likely to come later. A dozen migrating mallards had waddled down to the water from their resting place in Michael's yard and were now bobbing around the canoe as though they were contented rubber ducks in a bathtub. Early rays of sunlight struck the opposite shore in streaks that made the pines shimmer. Between the two shores, the water lay in silver stillness. Morning birds called to one another and darted through the woods.

"Oh, my…" Cassie said. After all of her dreams, after all those years of *believing,* she was finally on her way. Her fingers fairly itched to find the enchanted village that lay beyond the opposite shore.

Her smile started from the inside out. She could no more suppress the joy and anticipation that bubbled from within her than she could have stood on her head in the unstable canoe.

Swiveling to look over her shoulder, she said, "Isn't this the most glorious day you've ever seen? You're so lucky to live here year-round."

Michael feathered his paddle through the water. The radiant look on Cassie's face slammed up against his heart in an unwelcome way. Her fair cheeks were flush with excitement, her eyes wide with unabashed wonder. The blue life jacket he'd insisted she wear dwarfed her, hiding the subtle uplift of her breasts, but couldn't for a minute suppress her enthusiasm. She was off on a grand adventure. For an instant Michael regretted he was going to haul her up short, then quickly decided he didn't have room in his life for a woman like Cassie Seeger. Not even for a few wasted days.

"You'll paddle better if you face front," he said, his tone more gruff than he had intended.

"Oh, sure. I didn't mean for you to do all the work." She jammed her paddle into the water with more vigor than skill. "It's just that now that I'm actually here I want to savor every minute. I'm going to remember this trip for the rest of my life and I don't want to miss a single thing. Besides, I'm going to have to tell everybody back home all about it. Every detail."

The spray from Cassie's inept stroke showered Michael in the stern of the boat. The woman was her own worst enemy. With her lousy technique and her mouth working nonstop she was going to wear herself out in the first half hour. Of course by then Michael would be drenched. Though the temperature was pleasant enough, he wasn't eager for a skin-deep soaking.

"Cassie, this isn't a speed contest and you're not mixing up a vat of pancake mix. Go easy." He knelt comfortably in the bottom of the boat to gain maximum leverage with the paddle. "Watch me a minute."

He demonstrated with a few smooth strokes, first on one side of the canoe and then the other. "You can sit, if you want, instead of kneeling, but you have to use your lower arm as a pivot. Don't pull with it or your shoulder muscles will wear out. And don't yank the paddle so far out of the water after every stroke. It's a waste of energy and you splash me when you do."

"Sorry. I didn't realize." Cassie watched in fascination as Michael spoke. The Australian bush hat he wore, with a jaunty curve to its brim, cast a sharp shadow across his rugged features. He was all supple motion and power, the corded muscles of his forearms flexing with each stroke. There was something blatantly masculine about his effortless motions, and her gaze was drawn to his well-honed physique. His broad shoulders he earned by hard work, not pumping iron in a gym. His shirt stretched across the breadth of his chest, recalling the rock hardness she'd caught a tantalizing glimpse of that morning. Amazingly, his hands held the paddle in a firm yet gentle grip that was almost a caress. She couldn't help but wonder what it would feel like to have those same hands holding her.

Her interested survey dipped a bit lower and she felt a perverse sense of disappointment to discover his fly was firmly snapped closed. *Shame on you, Cassandra, for even thinking such a thing!* she admonished herself with a barely suppressed giggle.

"And the way to enjoy canoeing is to listen... not talk."

The sting of his words was like a slap, and she winced. "My talking really bugs you, doesn't it?"

Michael caught the hurt look in her eyes and cursed himself. When had he become so damn insensitive? Particularly since Cassie's voice had a melodic quality that was anything but irritating. The opposite, in fact—which was the problem.

"I've spent the last couple of years alone," he admitted. "Guess I'm not used to having company."

She nodded and turned around, dipping her paddle into the water with a much smoother stroke this time. Fast learner, Michael concluded. With a thin shell. So open and eager to please, she could be easily hurt, he realized. That made her vulnerable. And he was an oaf to have cut her off like that.

After a few moments of silent paddling, she quietly asked, "What do you recommend I listen for?"

My apology, he thought with a mental groan.

CASSIE VOWED NOT TO LET Michael's surly attitude bother her. A long time ago her Aunt Myrtle had taught her no one had the power to upset her if she didn't let them. A person had a choice of being happy or sad, she'd explained, so why on earth would anyone choose to be miserable?

Besides, Michael had a good point.

The canoe slid through the water with a soothing hiss and tiny wavelets lapped against the hull, sounds so subtle she'd miss them if she didn't listen hard. An adventurous bumblebee made his way to the middle of the lake, buzzed around the canoe and headed off in a new direction. From the south shore, Cassie could hear the distant sound of a chainsaw at work and the occasional shouted voice carrying through the still air.

A couple of other canoes appeared on the lake, their wakes glistening threads in the sunlight, the muted conversations of the occupants floating softly across the water.

Her secret grin grew wider by the minute. Cassie decided Michael could be a grouch if he wanted to, but she was going to enjoy every sight and sound the good Lord had provided.

She was acutely aware of the man sitting only a few feet behind her, however, just the other side of their neatly stacked gear, all of it stuffed into blue portage packs. She sensed how he matched his long, powerful strokes to her less confident rhythm, keeping the craft on a steady course. Knowing he was there, in her imagination his eyes on her back, sent a warm glow of longing through her. Searching for Way Quah with a man like Michael was a thrill she hadn't anticipated.

Surely she must have misunderstood what he'd said about killing his wife and child.

THE LAKE NARROWED into a shallow cove where the reflection of firs and pines along the shore cast the water in a deep shade of green. The sun was high now, beating down on the back of Cassie's neck. Sweat dampened her cotton shirt beneath the bulky life jacket. Her arms and shoulders had begun to ache with the constant, unfamiliar effort of paddling. Her legs felt cramped and her buttocks were sore from the hard seat. But she wasn't about to admit to Michael she needed a rest; she might be small but she was tough.

"Fun's over," he announced, the sudden sound of his voice startling her. "Coming up on the first portage."

That sounded good to her. She'd be happy for the chance to stretch her legs. "How far do we have to walk?"

"Two miles. We'll need to make a couple of trips to get all of our stuff to the other side."

Cassie suddenly realized he was talking about a six-mile hike, not a casual stroll through the woods. "No problem," she announced with a smugness she didn't feel. "I walk that far every day at work."

Michael floated the canoe alongside the bank with considerable precision.

The last thing Cassie wanted was to have him think she couldn't carry her own weight on this expedition. She swung her feet around, stood and picked up one of the heavy portage packs. Without thinking, she tossed it toward the shore.

His warning shout barely registered before she realized her mistake. Too late. She'd failed to take into consideration that on the water every action caused a reaction in the opposite direction . . . and hers was to tumble backward out of the boat.

Arms akimbo, she landed with a splash in two feet of water. The sudden cold made her gasp. Catching her breath, she looked up into dark, amused eyes.

Amusement at *her* expense!

"Don't you dare laugh at me, Longlake," she warned, stifling a giggle before it could erupt.

His lips twitched and engaging crinkles formed at the corners of his eyes. "No, ma'am."

Cassie knew if he gave her a full-fledged smile she'd be totally lost. "A gentleman would offer a lady a hand."

Using far more caution than she had shown, Michael stepped out of the canoe into the water. His lips still threatening to curl, he extended his hand.

His fingers were long and tapered, darkly tanned, his palm slightly rough and very masculine to the touch. And warm. So warm the heat arrowed up Cassie's arm and wrapped itself around her chest. Her gaze locked with his. She watched in amazement as his amused expression changed into something quite different, something hot, insistent and unexpected. It took her breath away and made her feel acutely feminine.

Michael's throat locked at the touch of Cassie's hand. She was soft. So soft. And he knew the rest of her body would be equally soft and silken. Need exploded in him, drawing every muscle painfully taut. When she stood, her jeans clung to her slim thighs like a second skin. Though she was petite, she had good, lithe legs. Strong legs. And he didn't want to think about how those legs would feel wrapped around his middle.

Before he could say or do something stupid, he escaped into the mental isolation he'd used for the last three years to ward off the pain.

"It's customary in this part of the country to get out of the canoe onto the bank, Cassie. You might want to give it a try next time."

"I was only trying to help." Embarrassment and anger flamed Cassie's cheeks. Boy, had she read him wrong! It hadn't been desire she'd seen in his eyes. Not even close.

She sloughed past him through the water and climbed up the bank, her boots slipping on the mud. From the canoe, she snatched up the pack that contained her change of clothes and headed off into the woods. She'd be darned if she'd wear wet jeans the rest of the day.

The secluded spot she found immediately lifted her spirits. A carpet of purple asters covered the forest floor beneath a stately white pine. The branches marched at an irregular pace up the trunk, reaching for the brightness of the clear sky.

Cassie sat down on a rock and pulled off her boots. How could anyone feel miserable for long in a place like this? she wondered.

When she returned to the lakeshore, her steps felt lighter. She'd get a smile, a real smile, out of Michael before this trip was over. She'd had plenty of experience handling grouchy customers, changing their moods and ending up with a big tip to boot. He was simply the same kind of challenge.

She found him sitting with his back against a granite boulder, staring darkly across the lake they'd just traveled. For a moment he reminded her of a Vietnam vet who came into the coffee shop when he had enough change for a decent meal. Pain haunted the depths of Jack's eyes in much the same way as Michael looked now. She wondered at the kind of sorrows he must have endured to wear his burden so heavily.

"Sorry I made a fool out of myself," she said with an intentionally cheerful grin. She plopped herself down next to him and picked out a sandwich from the plastic container on the ground. Bologna and cheese. Not exactly her favorite. "Guess we novices can be a real pain for an expert like you."

"You didn't know."

"I do now."

Michael cast her a puzzled look from beneath the brim of his hat. She was taking his rudeness too much in stride . . . her eyes bright, her smile a bit too pleasant. That gave Michael an uneasy feeling in the pit of his stomach. She had him off-balance. Had since she first showed up at his workshop. Something was going on in that busy little mind of hers. He suspected it meant trouble.

Perhaps trouble went with that sassy little turned-up nose of hers, a nose that had already been duly kissed by the sun. He should have reminded her to put on sun block to protect her fair skin, or better yet, wear a hat.

She certainly wasn't fussy about what she ate. Any guide worth his salt would have put together a hearty shore meal that would stick to a fisherman's ribs. Michael had taken the easy way out. If she had any sense, she'd have him blackballed from ever guiding again. Which wouldn't bother him all that much, he admitted. He'd given up that side of the business years ago. When there'd been no one to share successes and failures with, he'd simply lost interest.

After they finished the brief meal he stuffed the remnants of lunch back into the pack.

"Ready to go?" he asked.

"Sure. When you've got something tough to do, no time like the present, my aunt always used to say."

With a twinge of guilt, Michael wondered what Cassie's aunt would think about the dirty trick he had in mind. "The canoe weighs a lot less than the packs do. You want to try portaging the boat?"

"If you think that's best." She stood, dusting off her jeans right where the fabric curved into the shape of her thigh. Michael had to stifle a new surge of guilt along with a tightening of his loins. Why hadn't she read enough books at her damn library to know that packs were a hell of a lot easier to handle than canoes—particularly on the trail he planned to travel?

As the weight of the canoe settled on Cassie's shoulders, she decided Michael was right. The sleek craft was as light as a feather, at least far lighter than most of the trays she carried at the coffee shop. Of course, the darn thing stuck out a mile front and back, and felt a little unsteady, kind of flopping up and down with each step she took, but she supposed she'd get used to that.

Her vision was severely impaired, too. About all she could see were her feet and a yard's worth of muddy trail lined by leafy green ferns.

She'd barely gotten away from the shore when the canoe slammed into something, throwing its weight back onto her shoulders with a force that almost drove her to her knees. She gasped at the sudden pain.

"Keep the bow tipped down," Michael ordered from in front of her.

"Right." She took a deep breath to steady herself. "I remember the guys at my high school bragging about this kind of a trip. I was so envious. I'll get the hang of it in a minute."

But a minute later the path took a sharp turn to the right that she didn't see until it was too late. She, or rather the canoe, slammed into another tree. She staggered under the impact.

"Are you okay?" Michael asked.

"Fine." She wrestled the bow of the canoe out of the branches and started off again. "How is that heavy pack?"

"I'm managing."

She could have sworn she heard a smile in his voice; she must have been mistaken. And she didn't have much time to give to the thought because the stupid canoe got hung up again before she went ten more feet. She wrenched it free. In the process, she stepped ankle deep in an oozing puddle of mud.

A fine sheen of sweat covered her face. Along her jaw and between her breasts, perspiration trickled down. The farther they went into the woods, the more bugs they managed to stir up... little dinky things she called "no-seeums" that got in her mouth and eyes and tried to crawl into her ears.

And the mosquitoes. Good grief! They were having a banquet on her arms and neck and face.

"Michael! I've gotta stop," she pleaded.

He turned around to see her shrugging the canoe from her shoulders. As she dropped the awkward load to the ground, there was a wild-eyed look about her that frightened him. Could he have pushed her too far already?

"The bug repellant," she said with a catch in her breath. "It's in my carryall back where we landed. I've got to—"

Grabbing her arm, he restrained her hurried retreat back the way they had come. "Here. I've got some."

He handed her a small container of oily lotion. Frantically, she poured some on her fingertips and spread it across her forehead, down her cheeks and along the slender column of her neck. In spite of his desire to remain remote, Michael wished he could touch her that way, his hand exploring her smooth complexion, the delicate shape of her jaw, and venturing to that sensitive place that rested just below her ear. If she ever realized this walk in the woods had been entirely unnecessary, she would hate him. Already, angry red welts were apparent on her cheek and neck.

Damn! He ought to call this whole thing off. He should have put up with his grandfather pounding on his tom-tom for a month rather than putting Cassie through this ordeal.

But before he could articulate his thoughts, she gathered strength from somewhere, hefted the canoe again and announced, "Let's go."

The woman had more spunk than good sense. "I'll take the canoe."

"No. I'm okay. Really."

Stubborn as a mule, too. Against his will, Michael found himself admiring Cassie Seeger.

BY THE TIME CASSIE had finished the second trip through the woods, this time with a sixty-pound pack on her back, she had concluded her Aunt Myrtle had never truly understood misery. Cassie's shoulders and legs ached. She was hot and tired, stank of bug repellant and had moved beyond cranky.

But the view of the second lake was even more spectacular than the first. On the opposite shore, birch trees stood out starkly like white flagpoles in a mat of deep green. Along one barren branch, a row of sea gulls, looking out of place so far from the Great Lakes, waited on their perch to catch a glimpse of dinner surfacing in the broad expanse of water below them.

Heaving a sigh, Cassie settled herself on a fallen log near the shore. It was cooler there and a light breeze fanned her overheated face, clearing the area of bugs in the process.

She rubbed her hand along the back of her neck, resisted the urge to scratch a mosquito bite, then lifted her camera to her eye. Eldyne Bowen, one of the coffee shop regulars, had insisted Cassie needed a camera to record her expedition. All of the great explorers had documented their finds, she argued, so she had loaned Cassie this camera that had once belonged to her late husband. Who knew what might happen? Maybe Cassie would get her pictures published in one of those nature magazines.

Cassie adjusted the telephoto lens and snapped a shot of the birds across the way.

When she lowered the camera she noted a canoe rounding a rocky point off to her left. She stood and waved. The passengers returned the friendly greeting and headed in her direction.

Over her shoulder she called to Michael, who was setting up their campsite, "We've got company coming."

Watching the visitors approach, she had the strangest feeling they were in one of the boats she'd seen early that morning on Gunflint Lake. Of course, that wasn't possible. To get to this lake, they would have had to portage through the woods just as she and Michael had. They certainly would have met on that narrow trail.

The guy in the back of the canoe held up a good-looking string of a half-dozen smallmouth bass. "The fishing was great in the river back there," he called from just offshore. "Did you give it a try?"

River? What river? she thought with a frown. "No, we haven't tried our luck yet." They hadn't had time. "Maybe tomorrow."

"Well, good luck," the young man said. "We're gonna camp down at the far end of the lake. Check with you later." He gave another friendly wave and the canoe resumed its glide along the shoreline.

Cassie turned to Michael, who had joined her to greet their fellow travelers. He stood close enough so she caught his masculine scent, a heady combination of virility and pine that managed to accelerate her heartbeat whenever he came near.

As she looked at him, a niggling suspicion burrowed into the base of her spine. Something about his expression reminded her of a little boy caught with his hand in the cookie jar.

"Is there something you haven't told me?" she asked.

Michael tucked his fingertips into his hip pockets. Getting out of this one wasn't going to be easy. He hadn't counted on another canoe showing up. "Why do you ask?"

"Because, unless my eyesight is failing me, I saw those two guys in that boat this morning. And they were behind us. How did they get here before we did and have time to catch all those fish?"

He shrugged his shoulders in answer.

"Michael Longlake, is there another way to get here besides hauling all our stuff through the woods?"

"Well, yes," he admitted. "There is a run through a connecting river between the two lakes."

The color on her sunburned cheeks deepened and her eyes narrowed. "Then why did we spend hours stomping through the woods?"

He sighed in defeat. If he was going to end this trip, and end it in a hurry, he guessed he'd better tell the truth. "Because, Cassie, I don't want to be here. I told you that from the beginning. There's no mythical village, no Way Quah, no enchanted anything out there. I figured if I made the whole ordeal hard enough on you, you'd give it up and we could both go home."

If looks could kill, she would have nailed him on the spot, no doubt about it.

Chapter Three

Righteous fury rose up in Cassie.

"What in the name of sweet peace did I ever do to you?" She planted her fists on her hips. "This is the first time in my entire life I've ever taken a vacation. Shoot, it's the first time I've been more than a hundred miles from the Twin Cities. And here you go, tryin' to sabotage the whole thing. I just hope when all this is over you're not expecting a big tip."

She stomped up the hillside to where they had stacked their gear, delved into one of the packs and ripped open a box of Hostess Twinkies. She'd earned it, she thought grimly. This time with the sweat of her brow.

"If you were so intent on this vacation of yours," Michael challenged, "why didn't you make reservations with a proper guide?"

She whirled. "I did. The guy I signed up with had an emergency appendectomy the day before yesterday. I didn't know until I got to Grand Marais. What was I supposed to do?" She bit off a hunk of sweet confection. "This was the only time Arletta—she owns the coffee shop where I work—could let me get away. I can't go back empty-handed. What will all my friends think? That I make promises I can't keep? That I'm a quitter?"

"No, I doubt anyone would think that of you, Cassie."

In spite of her anger, something about Michael's low, intimate tone gave her a warm feeling right down to the tip of her toes. She tried to ignore the sensation. "So? Are you going to take me back to Gunflint now?"

"We'd never make it back before dark. Too dangerous. We'll have to spend the night here."

Why did she feel as though she'd just received a reprieve? Albeit a temporary one. "In the morning, then?"

"I think that's best."

She gobbled another bite of cake. "When I get back, I'm going to rent my own canoe, you know. I'm going to find Way Quah. No one is going to stop me." She didn't give up easy.

"Cassie..." He said her name in the most exasperated way, then threw up his hands in a sign of defeat. "I'll set up camp."

"I'll gather firewood."

"You don't have to do that. I'm your guide."

"Some guide! This was supposed to be a canoe trip. Not an exercise in how much of a fool you could make me feel."

"If I said I was sorry, would it help?"

She eyed him a moment, noting his casual stance, his legs wide apart, his thumbs hooked in his pockets so his hands framed his lean hips, the way the denim fabric pulled taut across his pelvis and the bulge where his...

Swallowing hard, she dragged her gaze upward, past the open collar of his shirt that gave her a glimpse of bronze skin, to meet his dark eyes. It wasn't easy for macho guys to apologize. She knew that. But she wanted more.

"What would help is for you to keep *your* promise to take me to Way Quah."

He shook his head. "You're like a dog working an old bone. You just won't leave it alone."

"Maybe I've had to be that way to survive."

She was a survivor, all right, Michael agreed. Hardheaded. Stubborn. Without the good sense God gave a tadpole. He also had the feeling she was like one of those blow-up punching bags he'd had as a kid. You could hit it as hard as you liked, rock it back on its heels, but it always popped up again.

He wasn't so sure he was half as resilient. Certainly his dreams weren't.

Trying not to think about the past, much less the future, he went about the business of setting up the domed tent on a level piece of ground near the fire pit. He didn't object when Cassie dragged in a load of downed wood to their campsite and only winced a little at her amateurish efforts with the ax to cut the logs into usable lengths. She wielded the tool with such intensity he wondered if she had her own demons to fight. As determined as she was to do her fair share of the work, he was grateful he'd brought along his emergency medical kit. One false swing of that ax and he was likely to need his paramedic training.

As he worked, he wondered if Cassie approached everything in her life with the same dedication. More precisely, he wondered if she made love with the same vigor she summoned for this little adventure. Not that he ever intended to find out. Before his marriage he might have taken advantage of the situation and hit on Cassie. But not now. The risks were too great.

He tossed the bedrolls inside the tent, zipped up the flap, then prepared to make dinner.

With experienced ease, he browned canned new potatoes in bacon fat in the skillet, adding sliced onions and corn beef to the mixture. The sizzling aroma reminded him it had been hours since lunch.

BY THE TIME they'd eaten and cleaned up the dishes, the last of the sun's rays had streaked a high-altitude contrail with orange, then slipped out of sight beyond the next ridge. The narrow lake lay as still as black glass. Silence pressed in around the lingering flames of the campfire, the only sound a soft hiss of sap escaping from a log and a distant frog announcing his search for a mate.

"How can you eat that stuff?" Michael asked from his spot on the opposite side of the fire.

Cassie looked down at her Twinkie, her second since dinner. "I'm a junk-food junkie." Particularly when she was upset.

"Your figure doesn't show it."

She suppressed a flutter of pleasure at what she took to be a compliment. He had the darnedest way of getting under her skin just with the sound of his voice. "According to my Aunt Myrtle I have the metabolism of a hummingbird."

A match flared. She watched as Michael pulled the flame in to the black stone bowl of his pipe. Smoke escaped from his lips and the rich aroma of tobacco mixed with wood smoke.

"A peace pipe?" she asked, half in jest.

"An old Indian custom. My ancestors used to think smoking was a way to send up prayers to the gods. I've always suspected the truth was the smoke kept the bugs away."

"I could have used some of that this afternoon."

The tobacco glowed as he drew on the pipe again, his lips closing lightly around the pipe stem. He blew out a stream of smoke, and she wondered what kinds of prayers Michael might be sending skyward.

"Sorry about your rugged initiation. Have you got some lotion for those mosquito bites?"

"Calamine. They don't itch too much."

Though she couldn't see him clearly, Cassie had the impression he was studying her across the fire. She squirmed under his careful scrutiny, adjusting her position against the log she was using for a backrest. To her great dismay, she wished she could cross to his side of the fire and sit with her head propped on his shoulder. She couldn't imagine a more romantic setting—the stars beginning to show through the tree branches, a soft rustling of little creatures in the woods, and a man unlike any she had ever met. There was a leashed sensuality about him, as though he fought to control the primitive side of his nature.

"Why are you so obsessed with Way Quah?"

There was no accusation in his voice, only curiosity. He spoke softly as though he didn't want to disturb the night.

Before she answered, she pulled her knees up to her chin and wrapped her arms around her legs.

"When I was a kid I had really bad asthma. I couldn't go out to play with my friends so I read voraciously. Everything I could get my hands on. The newspaper. The back of cereal boxes. Junk mail. The local librarian began to think my aunt was a shareholder. Somewhere along the way I got hooked on myths and legends. You know—Helen of Troy, the wee fairies of Ireland, Pegasus, and folks who try to fly to the sun on homemade wings."

She picked up a twig and started doodling with the tip in the fine gray dirt by her foot. "At some point my interest focused on lost civilizations, with a few hidden treasures thrown in for good measure. I dreamed about discovering Atlantis. Or finding Cíbola. All from my padded seat by a window where I could look outside and see other kids play."

"You must have been very lonely," he said.

"Not really. I had my dreams. And I *believed*. Oh, how I believed, and I still do."

"In Way Quah."

"Yes. So did my Aunt Myrtle."

The silence filled with his unspoken curiosity.

"My aunt died a little over a year ago," Cassie continued, fighting the sadness that washed over her. Her aunt wouldn't want her to cry over what couldn't be changed. "She'd been real sick for a long time. Most days there at the end she didn't even know me. I tried..." A thickness in her throat made her voice hitch. "Just before she died she looked up at me, and for a minute everything seemed to be okay. Like she'd come back from wherever she'd been. Then she said, 'Follow your dreams, Cassandra.' She said it just as clear as I'm talking to you. Then she closed her eyes real peaceful like, and passed on. I figure Aunt Myrtle knew what she was talking about." And recently Cassie had discovered an even more important reason to seek the pot of gold at the end of the rainbow, the special promise of Way Quah.

In the quiet that followed, Michael lifted a stick of dry pine from the woodpile and placed it across the hot coals. As the flame caught, he saw a reflection of his youthful vision. Brown, bare-bottomed toddlers playing happily at the entrance to their birch-covered wigwams; young mothers chatting as they parched wild rice in woven containers; the slightly out-of-focus image of a young girl he would someday love. He blinked the image away.

If nothing else, he understood Cassie's grief for her aunt. "Not many people have even heard of the enchanted village."

"As myths go, I guess it's not on any top-ten list."

"So why didn't you go in search of Atlantis, instead?"

Her soft, wistful laughter drifted around the campsite and lapped against Michael's heart, wearing away at the rock-hard barrier he had erected there a long time ago.

"Do you have any idea how much money it would take to launch that kind of an expedition?" she asked. "And all the technical equipment you'd need? You'd have to have a dozen bankers up your sleeve to pull that off. Northern Minnesota is a whole lot closer and a zillion times cheaper."

"Do I detect a practical streak in that otherwise fanciful head of yours?" As he teased her, he felt the corners of his mouth twitch. He hadn't indulged in playful bantering with a woman in a good many years. Somehow he felt rusty.

"Make fun if you want but I'll have the last laugh. You wait and see."

If determination alone would assure the outcome, Cassie was a sure bet to accomplish the impossible. For a moment Michael regretted he wouldn't be there to see her heart-stopping smile of victory.

Realizing where his thoughts had taken him, Michael sat back on his haunches. This woman was making him as crazy as she was. There was no Way Quah, no enchanted village. The tales had no more substance than ghost stories told around a shadowy campfire to frighten small children. Or dreams that turned into nightmares.

Cassie stretched out her legs, stifling a groan. She was beat. Muscles she hadn't been aware existed were making their presence known in her calves and thighs, and across her shoulders. There were a few matters she needed clarified, however, before she hit the sack.

"I don't want to appear ignorant," she said, "but I've noticed you only put up one tent."

"Sure. We'll have plenty of room. It sleeps four comfortably."

"Comfortably. Inside the same tent."

"I couldn't think of any good reason to haul two tents along." He stood and stretched, his long, jeans-clad legs highlighted by the glowing remains of the fire. His thighs looked rock hard. The denim fabric tugged tautly across his hips, and with electric surprise, she found herself fascinated by the ridge of male flesh that pressed against the zippered fly. A large man, she realized. Very large.

"Is there a problem?" he asked when she made no comment.

"No." The word stuck on a high-pitched note and she had to clear her throat. "No problem."

The problem was she had never slept with a man. Not all night. Not to wake up with him only inches away.

She wasn't a virgin. The temptation of Eddie Carter had been too much for her to resist, though in retrospect, the experience certainly hadn't come close to what she had hoped for. Indeed, she'd begun to wonder what all the fuss was about.

But she'd never in her life spent the entire night with a man. Much less with a *killer*.

She cleared the tightness from her throat again. "Before we call it a night, there's something I'd like to know. Did you really kill your wife and child?"

If he'd been jolted by a high-powered electrical current he couldn't have radiated more tension. "If you're asking if I stuck a knife to their throats, the answer is no. But as far as I'm concerned it was the same thing. The blame was mine, though the sheriff called it an accident."

Cassie felt his whiplash of pain as though it were her own. She started to go to him, to console him in some way, only to be halted in her tracks. In the glow from the firelight, two yellow eyes stared at her out of the darkness just beyond Michael's broad shoulder.

It was an eerie sight, mystical in its silence. Two golden lights shining in the vast blackness of night, as though from some other world, a place Cassie had only imagined.

"Michael." Her whisper caught in a hesitated gasp. "Behind you..."

As though awakening from a nightmare, he slowly turned. The shadowed figure beyond him shifted, and the outline of a deer appeared against the surrounding trees.

Cassie exhaled the breath she'd been holding. Nothing otherworldly there, no fanciful flight of imagination. Warm-blooded and real.

"We're probably camped on her usual trail to the water." Michael spoke so softly Cassie almost thought she'd read his thoughts rather than actually heard the words.

Shaking off the odd sensation that had raised the hairs on the back of her neck, Cassie said, "She's beautiful." The doe's coat looked rich and lustrous. She stood in a regal pose sniffing the air, her ears held at attention. "Why isn't she afraid of us?"

"She doesn't sense any threat. She'll move off in a minute."

Cassie would have liked the deer to stay forever. It was a magical moment, and that feeling was somehow magnified because she was with a man like Michael. Strong. Incredibly handsome. Surprisingly vulnerable. An intoxicating combination. She sensed in him a pain so great she wished she had the power to perform some kind of soothing surgery to make him all well again. But then, she'd always had an irresistible urge to "fix" things, and sometimes that simply wasn't possible.

In the distance a wolf howled, the sound echoing across the top of the forest canopy.

The doe bolted. She crashed through the woods, running away from the predator's call.

At the same frantic speed, a shiver traveled Cassie's spine as though ghosts were running across her grave. With frightening awareness she realized how isolated they were. If she and Michael were to travel together, each day would take them more distant from help. They would need each other in ways she hadn't fully understood. They would be forced to trust each other.

But because Michael didn't believe in Way Quah they'd never have that chance. She'd be traveling on her own.

For a long time, she didn't speak, and neither did Michael.

Finally, after quiet had settled again in the woods, Michael said, "Why don't you get ready for bed first. I'll make sure the fire is all the way out."

"Sure. I'll..." What was the protocol, she wondered, about telling a man good-night when you were about to sleep together? "I'll see you in the morning."

Michael waited until he saw the flashlight switch on in the tent. Then he turned away, bending to stir the coals in the fire pit. The way he was feeling tonight, as if he was riding an emotional roller coaster, he sure didn't want to watch Cassie stripping to her underwear, even in silhouette.

He berated himself for the way he had treated her. She was so filled with naive confidence that Way Quah existed, he hated to see her dreams shattered. It was going to break her heart. If he let her go off on her own there'd be no one around when she came face-to-face with reality.

He remembered the day the truth had struck him. *Dreams turn to nightmares. And the people you love most, die.*

He glanced toward the tent only to realize his timing was lousy. Unable to look away, he watched as Cassie raised her shirt over her head, which revealed the outline of her perky breasts. The garment dropped out of sight, then her hands reached for the waistband of her jeans.

He groaned and stabbed at the dying embers. His palms itched to cover her sweet shape, to lift and feel the soft weight of her breasts in his hands, to span her slender waist with his fingers. It had been so long, so very long....

He didn't have any pressing deadlines at the moment, he rationalized. A few days on the water wouldn't hurt one way or the other. He was due for some time off. Cassie would be a whole hell of a lot better off with him along than being on her own, particularly when she realized she was on a fool's errand.

Picking up a collapsible pail that sat beside the fire pit, he sprinkled water across the coals. Tomorrow he'd tell Cassie he had decided to guide her after all. He'd take her to that little white speck she'd seen on her map. And maybe hold her—just for a minute—when she discovered there wasn't anything there except more trees.

Wondering if she'd be pleased when he agreed to guide her, he glanced again toward their sleeping quarters.

With an effort, he suppressed a feeling of disappointment that all he could see was the dark outline of the tent.

"SHE IS AN OUTSIDER."

"She believes. That is all that is important."

"He was here once and now he has forgotten."

"He will believe again. She has the power to open his heart. I feel it."

"The tests are too difficult. If he doubts…and she falters because she is not one of us…all will be lost."

"We must have faith." Turning away from her rival, she lifted her child onto her lap, though because of her advanced pregnancy there was little room. She pulled the boy's head against her shoulder. Squirming, he fought to escape. After a single, quick hug she released him, smiling as he raced off into the woods.

Her husband placed a comforting hand on her shoulder. "This time, all will be well."

SLEEPING WITH A MAN wasn't all that difficult, Cassie concluded. Except for his heavy breathing. It wasn't quite a snore, but instead a deep masculine sound. That, along with the shifting of his body next to hers and the combined scent of wood smoke and man, had kept her awake for a good part of the night. In a strange way the whole experience had been both nerve-racking and reassuring at the same time. An odd sensation.

Cassie had been awake since the first rays of sunlight touched the tent. Michael's disturbing presence had driven Cassie from her bedroll and out to meet the new day. But not before she'd taken a quick glimpse of him, observing the way a lock of his midnight-dark hair had slipped boyishly across his forehead and his hard-angled features had softened with sleep.

Not a sight she should dwell on, she reminded herself. Far too dangerous. And futile.

She'd dressed quickly, pulling on the T-shirt her friends from Arletta's had given her. Surely the stenciled motto Way Quah Or Bust would keep up her spirits.

With her borrowed camera hanging by a strap from around her neck, she trudged up a hill in search of a high point with a view of the forests and lakes. Each time she drew in a breath, the fresh air tingled her lungs. The sky was a promising silver blue without a trace of clouds. As she ducked under branches and wove her way through the forest, the scent of pine and late-blooming wildflowers hung in the sweet-smelling air. Here and there she came across a lone maple or a stand of birch, trees that would provide a splash of bright color after the first cold snap.

High in the branches of a pine, a squirrel chattered and complained about her trespassing. A blackbird echoed the same complaint. Smiling, Cassie kept on moving.

What a glorious moment to be alive! Her chest tightened as she wished she could share her exhilaration with Michael.

If only he were a little more cheerful, she mused. Clearly, he took himself very seriously. She understood tragedy lashing out at a person and suspected that's what had happened to Michael. But she simply wasn't able to comprehend allowing the worst of life to mar all that was good. Her Aunt Myrtle wouldn't have permitted such self-indulgence.

She squatted to take a close-up picture of fireweed, its stalk filled with trumpetlike red flowers that had been kissed by dewdrops. Nearby, a scraggling white clover, thirsty for a serious rainfall, drooped its blossoms toward the ground. She squirmed her way beneath the plant and took the photo with the sky as a background. She knew Eldyne, who had loaned her the camera, loved flowers of all sorts and had a small garden of her own that would rival the best Minneapolis had to offer. Cassie vowed to bring home pictures that would please the elderly woman and perhaps ease, for a few moments, the grief she felt over the loss of her husband.

She wished she could bring home a bouquet of happiness for the woman, too.

In search of more wildflowers, she edged her way across a scree of jagged rocks. The footing was uneven. More than once on the steep slope she had to touch her hand to the ground to balance herself. With each booted step, rocks shifted and clinked against one another, disturbing the morning stillness.

A plaintive cry brought her up short.

Her gaze shifted across the terrain in search of the source of the whimpering sound.

Stuck between two slabs of rock, a young mink struggled for escape. He nipped at his captured paw, then clawed at the slate that had imprisoned him. Terror filled his wide brown eyes. His chest heaved with each frantic breath he drew.

He whined and struggled more fiercely as Cassie came closer.

"Ah, poor little baby," she crooned.

She shrugged off her light jacket. However innocent and frightened the mink might be, she knew he had sharp claws and razorlike teeth. He wouldn't know she was trying to help, at least not at first; instinct would make him lash out.

Dropping her jacket over the mink, she moved quickly to contain his efforts to escape while not letting the little creature hurt himself. A moment later she had him freed of the rocks and wrapped securely in her jacket.

Through the garment she did a quick inspection for injuries. His yelp of pain told her his foreleg was most probably broken.

"There's no help for it. I can't let you go," she explained in a soft, soothing voice. "The hawks or eagles would have you for dinner if I did. We've got to get that leg of yours all fixed up. That way you can be on your own again and find your way back to your mama."

Adjusting her camera behind her shoulder, she tucked her squirming bundle securely under her arm and headed back down the hill to the campsite. In a few moments, the mink's frantic efforts to escape eased and his trembling little body relaxed.

"Don't you worry, little guy. We'll have you fixed up in no time at all."

"I AM NOT GOING TO TRY to splint a mink's leg."
Michael cut Cassie a look that was meant to intimi-
date. It didn't do a damn bit of good. It wouldn't
with a woman who wore a powder blue T-shirt em-
blazoned with the words Way Quah Or Bust.

"But you told me you were on the rescue squad.
One little splint can't be that big a deal."

"I've had emergency medical technician training.
I had to because parts of the Gunflint Trail are pretty
remote, and those of us who winter here need to be
as self-sufficient as possible. But that training did *not*
include a course in veterinary medicine." The woman
was driving him crazy. Forget how his first deep
breath of morning air had included a whiff of her
wildflower scent, a tantalizing perfume that had him
on the brink of more than simple morning arousal.
He'd been grateful she'd hurried from the tent then.
No telling what he might have done if she'd hung
around a few minutes longer.

"Besides," he continued, "you shouldn't mess
with wild animals."

"He's just a baby and he's hurt. I couldn't very
well leave him out there all alone and crying." She
gave Michael a stubborn lift of her chin, which he
ignored.

"You never know what kind of diseases they might
be carrying. And minks bite, in case you hadn't
heard."

Holding the mink in her arms as gently as she might carry an infant, Cassie sat down on the ground next to the first-aid kit. Michael watched as the mink looked up at her with big, soulful brown eyes . . . as if he trusted her, for heaven's sake. She was darn lucky he wasn't taking a notch out of her finger. And if it weren't for the jacket wrapped around the animal's body, Michael was sure she would have long since been badly scratched.

Stroking the mink's head with a single finger, she said, "Ernie wouldn't hurt me, would you, sweetheart?"

"*Ernie?* What kind of name is that for a mink?"

"His eyes remind me of Ernie Schmidt. He's a really nice guy who has breakfast every Sunday at the coffee shop. Two eggs over easy, wheat toast, bacon and orange juice. Once in a long while he'll have oatmeal instead, but that's only when his doctor warns him about too much cholesterol. But a week or two later, he goes back to eggs. Since he's ninety-two years old and skinny as a rail, I'm not sure cholesterol matters a whole lot. What do you think?"

Michael's head spun. He didn't know what to say. They were supposed to be discussing whether or not to treat a mink's broken leg and suddenly he was learning the eating habits of some guy named Ernie.

Strangely, Michael found himself fascinated. Not with some old geezer who frequented a coffee shop in Deephaven, but with Cassie herself—the softness of her expression as she talked about the old man and the gentleness with which she held the mink. She was the same lady who had hauled a canoe over a grueling portage yesterday without complaint—until she discovered the effort hadn't been necessary!

A band of tension around his heart relaxed for the first time in years. As crazy as Cassie might be, she was an irresistible force.

He hunkered down in front of Cassie and the first-aid kit. "I think both Ernies are lucky to have you around," he admitted under his breath as he searched for a couple of tongue depressors to use as splints. "You're going to have to hold him real carefully. I'm likely to hurt him."

Cassie beamed Michael a smile that would have lit up a night sky. His lips twitched in response.

"I think he's figured out we're trying to help him," she whispered in a breath that warmed more than Michael's cheek.

Cassie felt little Ernie flinch at Michael's first touch, then the mink settled down with his cold nose buried at the crook of her elbow.

As Michael worked with careful, gentle hands, Cassie indulged herself by observing him up close. She was going to have to be sure to take at least one picture of him to show to her friends back home . . . and so she wouldn't forget a single detail—

the slight arch of his raven brows, the way his long lashes formed black fans on his bronzed cheeks and the sensuous curve of his lips. If he raised his gaze from the mink to hers, he'd find their faces only inches apart, their lips exactly opposite.

Would he think about kissing her? she wondered. It would take no more than an instant to bring their lips together to steal a quick taste. And how would she react if he did just that?

Eagerly, a knowing voice responded in her head.

She licked her lips and her mouth felt suddenly dry. She'd never been bold with men. She wasn't all that sure how to get a guy to kiss her when that was what she wanted.

But now she knew her nipples had begun to harden beneath her T-shirt and her breasts felt extraordinarily heavy. She ached to have Michael accidentally brush the back of his hand against her.

She could imagine the gentleness of his bronzed hands enclosing the white flesh of her breasts. His tapered fingers would feel rough on her skin; the contrast in texture and color was an electrifying thought.

Her pulse began to labor. Something about Michael stirred up needs in Cassie she had only vaguely been aware existed. She felt a compelling urge to touch him. With unfamiliar desperation she wanted to palm his cheek and feel the rugged angle of his jaw, the warmth of his flesh. Her fingers itched to plow furrows through his long hair, to feel its weight and texture.

She swallowed back a bitter sense of disappointment. He was taking her back to Gunflint today, and then she'd be on her own again. Not much chance he'd want to steal a kiss.

He lifted his head. In that instant she caught the heated look in his eyes and suddenly hope rekindled.

Chapter Four

Michael glanced up from bandaging the mink's leg to find Cassie staring at him. Her eyes were dark with what looked to be desire, and a rosy glow heightened the color on her cheeks like a morning sunrise.

Michael's loins tightened with a sudden surge of need. He wanted to kiss her.

As her tongue darted across her lips, moistening them, he focused his attention on her mouth. He imagined her sweet flavor and knew a soul-deep hunger he didn't dare acknowledge. It was more than just sex. As Snow Cloud had insisted, he felt a connection to Cassie he couldn't quite ignore but should. It was the smart thing to do.

"Cassie...don't look at me like that." His voice had a raspy quality he didn't recognize.

She swallowed and her tongue slid across the seam of her lips once again. "Like what?"

Because he couldn't help himself—he simply had to touch her—he lifted her chin with a single finger. With his thumb he rasped along the outline of her lower lip. The soft press of her flesh nearly undid him. "You're asking for trouble, Cassie Seeger. A wise woman would run like hell from me."

"I don't have to run. You're the one trying to get rid of me."

"Yeah. And what if I change my mind?" he threatened softly.

Her eyes widened and he felt her tremble. "I'd probably forget every bit of advice my Aunt Myrtle gave me."

"Such as?"

The corners of her mobile mouth quivered. "Like believing it when a guy tries to warn me off."

"Sounds to me like your aunt was one smart lady." Michael considered himself the fool as he leaned forward. One taste. That's all he'd take. He simply had to know for sure.

Her breath was warm and inviting on his face when something sharp bit down on his thumb. Hard.

He jumped back. "What the hell!" The mink had clamped his teeth around Michael's thumb.

"Ernie, don't do that," Cassie crooned, stroking the animal's head. "Michael is a friend. You mustn't hurt him."

Michael managed to pry his thumb free. Little spots of blood appeared on either side of the digit. "That's it! We're not going a single paddle length from this spot until you get rid of that mink."

"Don't be like that, Michael." She stifled a giggle and her blue eyes sparkled. "I think he's jealous."

"The hell you say." Sucking the blood from his wound, Michael stood and stared down at Cassie. He was lucky the damn mink bit him. The pain had brought him back to his senses.

He didn't want to get involved with Cassie. He didn't want to *care* about her or a little animal that didn't have enough sense to stay out of trouble. In spite of her current circumstances, Cassie was from the city. That was where women like her belonged. Not out in the wilderness, or living along a remote trail leading to nowhere. And his caring about her wasn't going to change that.

"Get your gear together," he ordered. "I'm going to prove to you that Way Quah is nothing more than a figment of somebody's imagination."

She raised her eyebrows. "You're going to take me there after all?"

"I'm going to take you to that nonexistent spot on the map you're so proud of. Only because my conscience would bother me if I let you go off on your own. And I don't doubt for a minute you're fool enough and stubborn enough to do just that."

"Thank you," she said coolly. "I'll take that as a compliment. But you needn't get yourself all in a lather, because I'm not taking one step away from this campsite in any direction unless Ernie comes along."

"Cassie..." Groaning, Michael speared his fingers through his hair. The woman was impossible. Fully as bullheaded as his grandfather. "I suppose you play the drums, too," he grumbled more to himself than to Cassie.

"No, not anymore. I used to when I was a kid but the noise got on my Aunt Myrtle's nerves." She frowned. "How did you know that?"

He rolled his eyes. "A wild guess."

The sun was already well up in the sky, dappling the campsite with shadows through the surrounding pines. At best they were getting a late start. If he stood there arguing with Cassie they might not get away till noon. Even then she was very likely to win, Michael admitted with a wry twist of his lips. Better to surrender now and get it over with.

"You'll have to make...Ernie—" he choked on the animal's name "—a nest out of one of the packs. We'll put him in the center of the canoe. Somehow we'll combine the rest of the stuff as best we can."

Her victorious smile brought another groan to his lips. She'd known all along he'd give in; she was as confident as his grandfather.

WHEN THEY HAD THE CANOE loaded, including Ernie comfortably settled in his ersatz throne, Michael squatted down on the beach and spread the maps out in front of him. With his hand compass he sighted along Cassie's map, drew two crossing lines, then did the same with his waterproof contour map. He circled the intersection in the maze of lakes and waterways, studying the shapes of the land and terrain carefully. This was no time to get himself lost.

Cassie peered over his shoulder at the contour map and felt a flutter of excitement in her middle. "That's it? That's Way Quah?"

"No, Cassie, it's just where your white spot is on the map. Probably a printing error. But that's where we're going so you can see for yourself."

She refused to be discouraged. "Interested in a little side bet?" she offered hopefully.

"You must be a serious gambler to want to make a bet like that."

"They tell me I shuffle a mean deck of cards."

He eyed her speculatively, his gaze lingering in a way that raised her temperature a notch or two. The hint of a predatory smile curled his lips. "How much are you prepared to risk?"

When he asked in that low rumblin' voice, what was she really prepared to venture? she wondered. Her heart? She'd never gambled in a high-stakes game like that before. The thought was downright frightening. Maybe for openers she ought to be a bit more cautious. "A kiss?" she suggested, startled by her boldness and the catch in her voice.

"That's not a very high price to pay if you lose. How 'bout we up the ante?"

She fought to control the forbidden thrill that curled through her midsection. "How 'bout we deal out a few cards first, then see how it goes? For all I know you may be planning to have me trudging across every portage from here to the North Pole."

"Not this time." He stood and folded the maps, then tucked them in a carrying case. "Straight as an arrow. No detours."

"Well, then, what if you get us lost? Sort of accidentally on purpose?"

"I won't. Not as long as I've got this compass." He extended his hand with the compass resting neatly in the circle of his broad, callused palm.

"I thought guides knew their way around these lakes."

"It's a big country, Cassie. One lake can look pretty much like another. There are all kinds of back bays and inlets, waterways so small they hardly show up on any size map. This is one little baby I never leave home without." He folded his tapered fingers over the plastic case, then slid the compass into his jeans pocket. "Let's get going."

As Michael shoved the canoe from the beach into the water, Ernie poked his head up on his long neck and looked over the gunnel, his eyes wide and his little ears twitching with anxiety.

"It's all right, baby cakes," Cassie crooned. "We're just going for a nice ride. You'll be fine."

Michael steadied the boat in the shallow water, offering Cassie his hand.

Their gazes locked for a heartbeat. Cassie wondered at the risk she was taking. Penny-ante poker on Thursday nights with her friends from the coffee shop seemed suddenly a much safer bet.

Swallowing her fears, she grasped his warm, masculine hand and stepped into the canoe. Surely one of her aunt's homilies had been something about *nothing ventured, nothing gained,* but for the life of her, she couldn't remember. Her thought processes seemed quite muddled at the moment.

As they pulled away from the shore, Cassie caught a movement out of the corner of her eye. Turning, she spotted a beautiful doe standing just inside the line of trees at the shoreline.

Quickly, she picked up her camera and snapped a picture.

"Michael, look. Isn't she lovely. Do you suppose she's the same doe we saw last night?"

He turned his head so the curled brim of his bush hat cast a sharp shadow across his forehead. With an easy movement, he lifted the hat and settled it more firmly in place. "Probably." Then he turned his attention to propelling the canoe down the length of the lake.

"THEY'RE COMING."

"They'll never find us."

"She has a map."

"Nonsense. It means nothing."

"She believes. That is enough. And the man has agreed to help her."

"They'll never pass the tests. There are too many, each one more difficult than the one before."

"She has already passed the test of compassion."

"That wouldn't have happened if you had disciplined your son."

"She is so kind she would have found another way."

PEACEFUL. That's how canoeing was supposed to be, Michael thought. Or maybe exciting, like when he drove his sleek craft through boulder-strewn rapids, white water spraying his face, the wind tossing his hair, and his muscles straining against the current.

Spending the day on the water with Cassie was a different kind of challenge.

The feminine slope of her shoulders filled Michael's view. Sunlight wove through the perky, blond strands of her hair, shining like polished gold before his eyes. The way she paddled with natural grace, if not expertise, fascinated him. He found himself waiting impatiently for the quick smile she tossed over her shoulder from time to time. His stomach knotted in anticipation.

In spite of calm water, this was not a peaceful canoe trip. Scattered clouds reflected back from the depths of the clear water, mocking him as two formless shapes merged into one, then separated again like mirrored lovers dancing across the lake.

He damned himself—and Cassie—for the unwelcome thoughts that kept entering his head. No mythical village was worth this kind of stress.

He even gave the mink a dirty look when the comical animal popped his head up to take a look around. It didn't do any good. The animal just looked back at him with those soulful brown eyes. Smirking, Michael thought.

At the approach of the canoe, a pair of loons resting on the water silently dipped out of sight, only to reappear a few moments later a hundred yards away.

Michael heard Cassie sigh as she lifted her paddle from the water and rested it across the gunnels. Water dripped from the tip, creating concentric circles that the canoe cut in half.

"Loons are special, aren't they?" she said, her smile wistful.

The knot in his stomach tightened. "I suppose."

"I mean, like they mate for life."

"A lot of birds and animals do. Bald eagles. Wolves." Humans, too, if they're lucky.

"I think that's nice."

"Yeah." He stroked his paddle firmly, making a J-shaped twist in the water to compensate for going solo while Cassie rested. He didn't begrudge her a break. She'd been doing her share all day. And he'd been going it alone for a long time... on the water and in his life. Maybe too long.

With the strength of will he'd developed in the last few years, he pushed away the sense of loneliness that often threatened to overwhelm him. He wouldn't burden Cassie by sharing his personal curse.

One of the loons dipped beneath the water again.

"My Aunt Myrtle never married. Claimed she'd never met a man she wanted to look at across the breakfast table every morning." Cassie pointed to the spot where the bird reappeared, off to the starboard side of the canoe. "But sometimes when we watched one of those old movies—you know, Fred Astaire, or Bing Crosby—I'd catch her crying at the mushy parts. Once I asked her about it."

"What'd she say?"

"She scrubbed at her eyes with the back of her hands and said she wasn't interested in going to a pity party."

Michael scowled. "Pity party? What's that?"

"You know. That's where you sit around feeling sorry for yourself. She didn't take kindly to that sort of thing, and told me so often enough when I was feeling blue over something or other I couldn't change." Cassie picked up her paddle again and dipped it into the water with a thoughtful shift of her shoulders. "Anyway, she turned off that old movie and made us a big bowl of popcorn. We played cards way past my bedtime that night, and she won nearly every game."

At the grim tone to her voice, as though Cassie had actually lost a real fortune, Michael's lips twitched. "She probably cheated."

Her head snapped around. "My aunt wouldn't..." The moment Cassie saw the glint in Michael's eye, she knew he was teasing.

Deftly, Cassie backstroked the paddle, cascading Michael with a fine sheen of spray.

"Hey, what are you doing?" he complained.

Getting even with you for picking on me. "Sorry," she said with saccharin sweetness. "Guess I'm not real good yet with this paddle."

"You're learning fast, sweetheart. Real fast," he grumbled.

But Cassie knew he wasn't mad. His lips were tilted into a half smile, and the corners of his dark eyes were crinkled with a faint trace of amusement.

It was enough to give her an unsettled feeling in the pit of her stomach, like going over the top of a roller coaster with no safety bar to hang on to.

She kind of liked the sensation. At least, where Michael was concerned. And it made her feel as if she'd brought a bit of light into the dark corners of his life, somehow eased the torment she occasionally glimpsed in his eyes.

As LUNCHTIME NEARED, Michael pulled the canoe up beside a rocky shore backed by a vertical cliff a hundred feet high.

"We've got a choice," he said, deftly using his paddle to hold the boat in place just offshore. "What you see in front of us is the remnant of a lava flow ten million or so years ago. Sometime after that, the land tilted and parts of it sank and others rose, leaving some rugged bluffs. On the other side of this one is the next lake we want, the one that will take us northeast toward your little white spot on the map." With his thumb, he tipped his hat farther back on his head. "We can either go up and over, or we can spend an extra day or so heading south and then come back around through a series of connecting rivers."

Cassie craned her neck to peer at the top of the cliff. The wall was so steep little vegetation grew among the rocks. Water seeped through some of the cracks and crannies, coloring the stone a dark green and making the sheer face look slippery. "You mean we have to climb that?" It made her dizzy just to look at it.

"That's the idea."

"With our packs and canoe and stuff? Ernie, too?"

"I'll go up first and lower a rope. You'll attach our gear and I'll haul everything up. Including you and the mink, if you need the help. It would save us a full day, maybe more."

She cut him a look. "You're not fooling me again, are you? If you make me climb that darn thing and then I find out—"

He held up his hand in a mock Boy Scout salute. "I told you, straight as an arrow. You want to go the long way, it's okay by me."

"But you'd rather go this way." And get the trip over with sooner, she suspected, trying to read his guarded expression. He never gave much away. She wished he would. It was so hard to deal with a guy when you didn't know quite what he was thinking. Why couldn't men be as up-front with their feelings as women? Sure would make life a heck of a lot less complicated.

"If I were guiding a group of guys we'd probably pick the shortest route."

That was a low blow to her pride that stiffened her spine. "Then let's get started," she agreed, lifting her chin. She wouldn't mention that dangling from the end of a rope a hundred feet in the air didn't sound like her idea of fun.

Tipping her head back, she caught a glimpse of movement along the top of the ridge. Something quick and gray, and ominous in the way it vanished from sight before she could quite identify if it was substantial or simply a shadow.

One of those shivers ran down her spine, the same as when she was a kid and walked by a cemetery filled with mossy headstones. In spite of the heat of the day, she wrapped her arms around herself.

Maybe she should have opted for the long way around.

Chapter Five

It took them a half hour to unload the canoe and eat a quick lunch. After giving Cassie instructions about attaching the portage packs and canoe to the rope, Michael began his ascent. He certainly wasn't interested in wasting time, she mused.

Because the noon sun was so warm, he'd changed into khaki shorts and a tank top. Hand over hand he climbed upward, moving with the same agility as a mountain lion, finding invisible handholds as easily as if he had placed them there himself. He made it look as simple as a walk in the park. His muscles rippled smoothly, like water flowing over rock. She watched with growing admiration the higher he went. Though he could hardly be described as muscle-bound, this guy was definitely a hunk. The kind of man who brought a roomful of women to instant awareness the moment he appeared.

She blew out a sigh. Wouldn't she love to walk into Arletta's café on Michael's arm. The folks back home would be tickled pink. So would she, Cassie admitted. More than that.

Without appearing to have built up a good sweat, he stood at the top of the cliff. When he removed his hat a slight breeze caught his hair, shifting the dark strands across his forehead. He shrugged off the coiled rope he'd carried slung around his body.

"Watch it, Cassie. Here it comes."

The end of the rope snaked through the air to land at her feet. "I got it."

Following his earlier instructions, she tied the rope securely around a center rib of the boat. She lifted the canoe, carrying it toward the spot he'd chosen as a direct drop from the top. He didn't want the fragile craft banging against the rocks. Neither did she.

With nothing but arm strength, he lifted the boat. It swung back and forth at the end of the rope like a slow pendulum, rising upward at a steady pace and making Cassie feel slightly sick to her stomach as she watched. She definitely didn't want to be in the same sort of fix.

The portage packs came next.

Then it was Cassie's turn. It wasn't as far as it looked, she told herself. If this was the kind of thing Michael's macho buddies could do, so could she.

She hoped.

She tucked a protesting Ernie into a carryall she slung securely over her shoulder. "Be quiet, baby cakes. I don't think I'm going to like this any more than you, but we've got no choice. You wouldn't want Michael to think we're chicken, would you?"

The mink whimpered and ducked his head.

As she looked up at the cliff, her courage fled. Moisture formed in the palms of her hands. She swiped them on her jeans.

"Just don't look down," she warned herself.

With the rope tied around her waist, she took a few tentative steps upward. It was easygoing at first. There were plenty of places for both her hands and feet. She was strong. She could do this. The rope tugged reassuringly around her middle. No sweat.

The wall in front of her face grew steeper. She caught the scent of dry rock. Ernie whined. Cassie's arms began to ache and tremble. Perspiration beaded her forehead and her mouth became dry. Now she really didn't like this.

"You're doing fine, Cassie," Michael called from above her. "Keep coming."

"Right." She tried for a bright and eager smile as she looked up. That was a bad mistake.

The gray-green wall of rock swam toward her in a totally disorienting way. She gasped. And then, as though possessed, the cliff shifted its position again. Back. Away from Cassie.

Her right foot slid off its precarious perch. The sound of pebbles pinged down the steep slope. She dug her fingers into any crack she could find. It didn't do any good. Her unbalanced weight dragged them back out again.

"No-o-o-o!" she cried, clawing frantically at the undulating cliff. The thing was alive. Fighting her. Trying in some spooky way to kill her. She could feel it shoving her back with a force that seemed evil. She caught its scent, like an egg that had been left to rot on the porch. Or maybe it was her own irrational terror she smelled.

She gritted her teeth and renewed her determination. Dammit, she wasn't going to fall. She was on her way to Way Quah!

The rope around her waist brought her up sharply. "I've still got you," Michael shouted. "Take it easy. You'll be okay."

His voice steadied her as much as the rope. Panic receded. Her foot found another perch, her fingers another hold. Solid. Unyielding. She moved upward another notch, trusting Michael as she had never trusted anyone else in her life. He wouldn't let her fall.

What she had felt was only fear, she assured herself. Only her imagination. A mountain couldn't be possessed, nor could it shift any direction of its own volition.

When she crested the top, Michael pulled her into his arms and she sagged against him. Every last muscle in her body felt as weak as rubber bands stretched too far, too long. In contrast, his body was like solid steel. Against her ear his heart beat steadily in his chest. She inhaled his musky, male scent. It simply wasn't fair she liked being in his arms so much when he was only in a hurry to finish their trip.

"You did good," he said, his voice low and surprisingly husky, as though he might have been worried about her.

"I think I may want to take the long way around next time," she confessed.

Michael kept her pressed up against him for a minute or two longer than necessary. He knew it wasn't smart to hold her this way. He'd already lost too many people he cared about, and he didn't want to start the same cycle all over again. And Cassie, he realized, would be easy to like. A lot.

"When I was climbing, did you..." Her voice cracked and she raised her head. "Did you feel any, well, you know...evil spirits, or anything like that?"

His breath lodged in his lungs. "No, Cassie. When you slipped, you panicked. That's all."

She smiled unconvincingly. Suddenly Michael wasn't so sure himself. If there really was a Way Quah...

But that thought was ridiculous.

BY LATE AFTERNOON they'd crossed another couple of lakes and wound their way through connecting rivers. There'd been only one more portage...a short one of no more than a couple of hundred feet on very level ground. Michael had carried the canoe.

Now they glided along a narrow strip of water sun streaked with diamonds. Birds darted through the treetops gobbling up their dinner of mosquitoes in an eating frenzy before darkness fell. Other birds swooped low over the lake to snatch hatching caddis flies in midair, and a kingfisher looked for larger prey as he cruised above the water.

A small splash in shallow water near the shore set up a circular ripple.

Michael lifted his paddle into the canoe. Nobody could resist an invitation like that, he thought. At least not any fisherman he knew. "Hold up, Cassie. Let's see if we can get ourselves a couple of small-mouth bass for dinner." With reeds growing out of the water and a couple of toppled pines for shelter, this looked like prime feeding ground for bass.

"We're going to fish?"

"Sure. I *am* a licensed fishing guide, you know."

"Well, sure, but I didn't think you'd want to take the time."

"Time spent fishing is never wasted." In a few swift motions, he'd put two spinning rods together, strung the lines and had the feathered lures attached. Truthfully, he'd rather be using a fly rod, but beginners had some trouble with that. And he wasn't a purist.

In the meantime, he'd noted a couple of other rises in the reeds. Big ones. This definitely had the feel of a hot spot. "Have you ever fished before?" he asked.

"Once. It was a kids' day at Lake Minnetonka." Cassie smiled wryly. "First time I cast, I managed to get my line tangled with some other kid's. He started to cry, so his mother came running out onto the dock real mad like and practically bopped me on the head with her purse. After they got that mess straightened out, I tried to cast again and my hook got stuck in the instructor's ear. Some other guy unhooked him, all right, and I don't think he was hurt real bad, but they asked me if I'd mind just watching for the rest of the day." She shrugged. "I didn't go back the next year."

Michael choked back a laugh. "We'll see if we can do better this time."

"Fine with me. But maybe you ought to keep your hat pulled way down over your ears."

"I'll consider myself forewarned." Her dazzling smile sent another kind of warning twisting through Michael's gut that put a good many of his senses on alert.

Handing her a rod, he said, "Watch me the first time. Then you can give it a try." Explaining the technique, he flipped the bail on the spinning reel and cast the lure right to the edge of the reeds where he'd seen the last rise.

"Good shot," she commented.

He gave two or three short jerks to the tip of the rod, making the lure imitate an injured minnow as he reeled in the line. But nothing rose to the bait.

"Okay. Your turn. When you get the lure in the water, don't let it sink to the bottom. It'll get tangled in the weeds."

"Got it."

It looked as if she was doing everything right. Except when Cassie let loose, the line spun around the tip of the rod a couple of times like a streamer on a maypole, then the lure dropped right into the middle of the canoe.

The mink screeched and there was a great flurry of claws scratching on fabric as he frantically tried to escape the twirling hook.

"Oh, baby cakes, I'm sorry!" She shifted her position to check on the animal. The canoe rocked precariously. "Did I hurt you, Ernie?" she crooned.

Michael grabbed for the sides of the boat. "Easy, Cassie. You're going to capsize us." She was a menace. But then, a lot of amateurs were, he reminded himself. "The mink's okay, but I think he'd rather *eat* fish than be hooked like one."

She grimaced. "I know."

"Let's give casting another try." And maybe Ernie would be smart enough to duck this time.

A few more attempts and Cassie finally got the line in the water, the lure right smack in the middle of the reeds.

"Reel in quick," Michael ordered, "or you'll get hung up on the bottom." And he'd either have to wade in after the lure or cut the line.

"I can't. It's stuck."

So much for lesson number one. "Maybe it'll come loose. Tug on it some."

"I am. It won't let go." The tip of the rod was bent in a deep arc, as though there was a ninety-pounder on the other end. Or more likely, a big log. "I'm sorry, Michael. Really I am. I guess I blew it again."

"Don't worry about it. A few snags come with the territory." He picked up his paddle. "Keep the line taut. I'll row us over there. Maybe I can pry the lure loose." He edged the canoe toward the reeds. They'd spooked every fish for a half mile with all the noise and activity, he was sure.

"Michael..." Cassie's voice trembled. "There's something...wrong!"

His gazed snapped from where the line arrowed into the water, up to the tip of the rod and back down again. The line was definitely moving farther back into the shallows. It couldn't be... "My God, Cassie, you've got a fish." A hell of a big one, from what he could tell.

"Oh, no! What'll I do?" she wailed.

"Just do what you've been doing. Keep that line nice and taut." He put the oar in the water and paddled backward at a steady rate. "You'll wear him out. Just don't let him get back under that fallen tree."

"Help me, Michael. I don't think I can—"

"Sure you can. Keep reeling in. Slow and steady." With one eye on Cassie and one on the fish, he worked the canoe to help her maintain the pressure. She was doing fine. And she wanted that fish. He could see her determination in the stubborn set to her jaw and the intense furrowing of her forehead. Someday she'd make a hell of a good fisherman.

"He's coming your way," he warned. "He's thinking about making a dash for deep water. Be ready to crank him in."

"Michael . . . I think— I can't catch my breath."

"Just relax. You've got everything under control."

To Michael's relief, she eventually worked the fish up close to the canoe. He was a big one, all right, maybe eighteen inches long and thick enough for fillets across the middle. A heck of a good catch for a first-time fisherman. Hell, a real keeper for anybody.

Cautiously, Michael lowered a long-handled fishing net into the water. This was one fish that wasn't going to get away. Not if he could help it. "Easy now," he urged. "Bring him this way. Just a bit."

With a quick scoop of the net, the fish came into the boat, his tail flailing.

Even though it was Cassie's fish, Michael felt as pleased as if he'd just caught a record breaker himself.

Her cheeks were flushed and her blue eyes sparkled. "Thank you, Michael," she said in a hoarse whisper. "I've wanted... Without you, I couldn't have..."

"You did all the work." Not an entirely true statement, but close enough.

She shook her head, smiling. "If I didn't think I'd tip us over, I'd crawl right on back there and give you the biggest darn kiss you've ever had. I swear I would."

"Yeah, well... maybe later." After the thick feel of emotion had cleared from his throat.

"Can we catch another one?" she asked. Her eyes were alight with the enthusiasm of instant addiction to the sport. "This one probably has a bunch of little brothers and sisters hiding back in the weeds. I'll even let you have a turn."

Michael checked the lengthening afternoon shadows. A row of dark clouds were beginning to build on the horizon. "We've probably scared them all away from this hole for now, and the one we've got is plenty big enough for the two of us. We'll save the rest for another time. Let's go find a campsite before it gets too late."

"What about Ernie? He's probably real hungry, too."

"Right. He's worked his fingers to the bone all day." Using a pair of long-nose pliers, Michael removed the hook from the fish. "Ernie will get his fair share. I promise."

Cassie beamed him one of her heart-stopping smiles. "You're beginning to like baby cakes, aren't you?"

Michael winced at the very thought. "About as much as a mailman likes a dog that bites."

"He's sorry about your thumb. I'm sure he is."

Ernie growled and bared his teeth.

"Sure he is. Only because he didn't bite it off at the knuckle."

"Now, boys," Cassie crooned. "Let's all be friends."

Michael wasn't convinced that was possible.

Following his instructions, Cassie unstrung her fishing pole and put it away in the carrying tube. One fish might not seem like much to anyone else, but this was her very first. And Michael had helped her catch it. She'd always treasure the memory of the pleasure she'd seen in his dark eyes.

Once they had the gear stowed again, they paddled along the shoreline to an outcropping of granite that would serve as a dock. Michael edged the canoe alongside, climbed out and hefted one of the portage bags onto shore. "How 'bout I take your picture with the fish before I clean it?"

"Would you?" Cassie unzipped a remaining pack to retrieve her camera. "Arletta and the others would think I was telling a tall tale about the size of the fish unless I had the proof. We've got one customer—Flossie Roosevelt—who's always tellin' wild stories about the monster pike she catches in the lake. Right from her own dock, she claims. But nobody quite believes her. They all figure she makes up the stories just to get attention. Which is okay, I guess, but I'd like them to believe me."

He steadied the boat for her as she got out. The customers at her coffee shop must be an odd lot, he thought, and he wondered if they were all as devoted to Cassie as she was to them. He figured they probably were. "This will convince 'em," he assured her.

A moment later, he posed her holding the fish. A column of sunlight gilded her complexion with a healthy glow. Her hair looked rich and vibrant, the sun tracing sparks of red among the tumble of fly-away gold strands. Staring through the viewfinder for longer than necessary, he let the image imprint itself in his memory. The eager smile that lit up her face. Subtle changes in light and shadow as they slid across the outline of her breasts each time she took a breath. The flare of her hips curving into shapely thighs.

Suppressing a groan, he snapped the picture.

"I'll send you a copy after I get home," she offered. "If you'd like."

"That's not necessary." He wasn't likely to forget Cassie. Not in the next hundred years or so.

"Oh." Cassie lowered the fish, her sense of disappointment a hurtful lump in her throat. Michael had no interest in her picture or, for that matter, in remembering her. Not that there was any reason he should, she reminded herself. He was definitely on this trip under duress. Still, he didn't have to make his feelings quite so obvious. "Mind if I take your picture, too? My friends will be interested in seeing my official boundary waters guide." The biggest catch of all, one Cassie had little chance of landing.

"Sure. Go ahead."

He handed her the camera and they switched places so the sun highlighted his face instead of hers. His hat was cocked at a jaunty angle, the brim rolled away from his face on one side, and his camouflage shirt open at the collar in a sexy, casual way.

"Could you smile a little?" she asked. *Just one. For the camera if not for me.*

"I thought I was." His lips twitched.

She snapped the picture. "It'll do."

"I'll clean the fish, and then I'll rig up the shower so you can bathe before dinner."

"You're kidding. We get to have showers?"

"Don't get too excited. It's not exactly like home. Just a makeshift affair with a bucket of warm water. But it's better than going in the lake. That water's pretty darn cold for bathing."

"Shoot, after a couple of days in the sun, a little rock climbing and a few gallons of bug repellant, anything resembling a shower sounds like heaven." She quickly stifled the thought that a shower for two would be even more thrilling.

From his place in the canoe, the mink whined a pitiful sound.

"Oh, Ernie, baby, I'm coming. I wouldn't forget to take your picture, too."

AN HOUR LATER, as the sun settled silently into the approaching clouds, Cassie stepped behind the tarp Michael had rigged for a modesty screen. True gentleman that he was, she knew he wouldn't peek. Darn it all.

In high school she hadn't exactly been the one the guys tried to spot through a hole they'd drilled into the girls' locker room. It hadn't mattered. She wasn't all that interested in them, either. Or so she'd told herself when she was fifteen. But she kind of wished time had improved her figure, at least enough to attract the attention of a man like Michael.

Above her, a bucket of warm water hung from a tree branch by a rope. A pull cord was attached to one side of the container to tip it as needed. Michael had assured her she'd be able to manage the contraption on her own. With a determined sigh, she decided there probably wasn't enough water for two, anyway. And she definitely needed a bath.

She shrugged out of her T-shirt, jeans and underwear, folded them neatly and lay them on a nearby rock that was covered with a painter's pallet of colorful lichen. She could hear the crackle of the camp fire and Michael moving around as he finished setting up camp. Beyond their little clearing in the forest, there wasn't another living human. The trees blanketed all sound. Only the scent of wood smoke drifted on the gentle air currents.

How far was Way Quah? she wondered. *How much longer would she be with Michael?*

Taking her soap in hand, she stood under the bucket. The air was cool on her flesh, the rocks uneven beneath her feet.

Gingerly, she pulled on the cord. A narrow stream of warm water cascaded over her head and across her shoulders.

"Hey, this is all right!" she called to Michael.

"Thought you'd like a few amenities."

She smiled, lathering herself with soap. "You sure I don't have to save any water for you?" Or make room for you?

"No thanks. I'm warming some more now for myself. I'll shower after you're done."

She supposed it wouldn't be fair if she sneaked a peek at him, since he was being so circumspect about a woman taking a shower only a few feet away from where he puttered around the camp fire. She imagined he had a wonderful body—lean and hard, with muscular legs that went on forever. Probably a cute butt, too. Not that she'd have a chance to find out.

Pulling the cord again, she let the water rinse her off, turning her head from side to side as the soapsuds slid off her hair, down her breasts and puddled at her feet. She wiped her hand across her face. When she opened her eyes, she froze.

A huge gray wolf stared back at her. A heavy coat of fur covered his muscular body. The bristles were raised along the back of his neck, and his tongue lolled out the side of his mouth. Beady eyes assessed her. For dinner, she thought uncomfortably.

"Go away, doggie." Though she'd tried for firm, her voice had come out in a squeak. She tried again. "Michael." The tightness in her throat pinched off the sound.

The wolf's lips pulled back into a snarl, revealing sharp fangs that seemed a foot long. He growled low in his chest, took a menacing step toward her, and she caught the faint scent of rotten eggs.

"Michael!"

Chapter Six

She flew at him like a wild woman. A *naked* wild woman, Michael mentally amended as Cassie threw herself into his arms. Before he could figure out what was going on, he had a quick, enticing vision of pert little breasts and a narrow waist.

"He's after me, Michael!" she cried. "Help me!"

He pulled her hard up against his chest, protecting her from whatever danger threatened. Or maybe she was the one who nestled up tight against him. Or maybe he'd been hoping for this kind of an excuse to wrap his arms around her again in the same way he'd briefly held her at the top of their rock climb. He could feel the press of her body along the length of his. Automatically his hand rested on the swell of her hips, her flesh cool to his touch. She trembled. Whatever else might be happening, she wasn't faking being frightened. And he was suddenly worried. Cassie Seeger was his responsibility. He'd once failed in his duty to another woman; he wouldn't let that happen again.

He scanned the campsite. "Who's after you? What are you talking about?" They were a million miles from nowhere and he hadn't heard a sound. He sure as hell doubted some crazed killer was on the loose this far north. Still, as his heart pounded in erratic sync with hers, he knew in her own way, Cassie was the one who was driving him crazy. She'd have that effect on a monk, he was sure.

"A wolf! Big and gray. I was taking my shower and he was watching me—"

"Watching?"

"So close I could smell him." Like this afternoon. Sickening. What the hell was going on? she wondered.

Just then a flash of gray crossed the campsite in a blur. The animal was so fast its outline was indistinct.

"There he goes." Relieved, Michael turned her so she'd see the predator running away. The swift animal vanished into the darkening forest with barely a sound.

"Oh, Lord . . ." Gasping for breath, still shaking, she rested her head on his chest. She was wet and slick and smelled of her special wildflower fragrance. It must be her shampoo, Michael thought dimly, his palm cupping the curve of her hip while he nuzzled her hair. So sweet. So long since he'd held a woman in his arms.

He forced himself to stay in control. A difficult trick, considering the painful ache in his loins. He felt battered by contradictory forces—his need and the fear that somehow by caring for Cassie he'd end up losing her.

"Cassie, you're safe now. The timber wolf's gone."

"I was so afraid."

"Yeah, I know." So was he, because of the things he was feeling and wanting and shouldn't even be thinking about. He gritted his teeth. He had to bring a halt to all of this. Now. Before he forgot, before the haunting memories dimmed and he could ignore the guilt he'd so rightfully earned.

"Cassie, have you noticed you don't have any clothes on?" Every part of Michael was painfully aware of her state of undress.

Cassie raised her head. Until that moment she hadn't been conscious of the press of her breasts against Michael's unyielding chest. Or the roughness of his jeans brushing against her thighs. Or the sweet feeling of his arousal hard against her abdomen. She'd been too scared.

But she knew now. In exquisite, glorious detail. The man wasn't a saint, after all!

From each point of contact, heat raced out in all directions, flushing her entire body with a blush that gave new meaning to the color red. The look in his eyes was almost as predatory as the wolf's had been—but far more welcome. His gaze focused on her trembling lips. This time, surely this time...

Abruptly, he released her and stepped back. He quickly shrugged out of his shirt and draped it around her shoulders from arm's length. As if she had the plague, she thought grimly.

"You'll catch a chill," he warned.

She wanted to swear out loud. *Good grief! Would it be so awful to kiss me? Once?*

"Thanks," she mumbled. Embarrassed by both her actions and her wayward thoughts, she pulled the shirt closed across her chest, a shirt that carried his special masculine scent. Of course, now *he* was bare from the waist up. That didn't do Cassie's plummeting spirits much good. Her fingers literally itched to touch him, to outline the smooth strength of the well-defined muscles across his chest, the ribbed flatness of his belly. A sweet torture of denial. "If you think it's safe, I guess I'd better get dressed."

He cleared his throat. "That's probably a good idea."

No, it was a dumb idea. She could think of a zillion others that would be a whole lot more fun. But the forbidden notions racing through her mind took two to make them work.

THE RAIN BEGAN SOMETIME during the night. The steady drip on the double roof of the tent became a heavy downpour by dawn. Wind shook the nylon fabric.

Waking slowly, Cassie rolled to her side. Onyx eyes looked back at her. Her heart did a little flip-flop and she smiled. What a nice way to start the day.

Remembering Michael wasn't very talkative first thing in the morning, she spoke softly. "Hi."

"Hi, yourself," he said in his raspy, morning voice.

"Been awake long?"

"A while."

"Oh." Looking at her? she wondered. "Sounds like it's pretty wet outside."

"Not a good travel day."

"I suppose not." Perhaps she should suggest some alternative activities. One idea popped immediately into her head, although she suspected he wouldn't be in the least bit interested. And that thought was becoming an old tape she ought not to replay again.

"Fish are probably biting."

"Really?" Not exactly what she had in mind, but it would probably have to do. "I've read how you're supposed to have fish for breakfast when you go camping.''

"Cooked over an open fire.''

"Soggy firewood a problem?'' In lieu of that, she'd be happy to reconsider her first choice of recreational activity.

"I think I can handle it.'' He sat up and speared his fingers through his dark, sleep-mussed hair.

Deliberately, she studied the curve of his back as he reached for his shirt. With quick appraisal, she memorized the breadth of his shoulders, and his smooth, bronzed complexion. She'd seen nude statues, a sculptor's concept of perfection, but she doubted any artist would be able to do Michael Longlake justice. He was simply too supple, too strong and pliable ever to be successfully imitated in anything as cold and hard as marble. And she mustn't think about how the warmth of his flesh would feel beneath her hands.

"Did you grow up always wanting to be a fishing guide?'' she asked.

"I suppose. At one point I was thinking about buying a lodge on the lake. I figured I'd do the guiding and my wife would...'' He lowered his head and his voice trailed off. "But it didn't work out.''

"How come! I know your wife died, but that doesn't mean you have to give up your dream.''

"Running a fishing lodge isn't something you can do alone."

"Well, that lady who owns the Lakeside Lodge is sure anxious to sell and move herself and her husband down to Florida. Guess neither one of them are feeling real healthy these days. Bet you could buy the place for a—"

"Leave it be, Cassie." He punished the laces of his boot by pulling them tight. "I don't have a wife to help me, and I have no plans to marry again. Ever. A woman doesn't belong stuck out in the middle of nowhere, without a prayer of getting proper help in an emergency. So there's no wife. No lodge."

"Oh." Cassie figured that was about the longest speech she'd ever gotten out of Michael, and she was sorry she'd butted into his business. She'd certainly gotten an earful. At least she knew exactly where she stood—nowhere. He wasn't even willing to *think* about getting married again.

"I'm sorry," she said. "Guess I'm always trying to fix other people's business when I should learn to keep my big mouth shut." She hadn't meant to push his misery button.

"Yeah." He visibly struggled to regain his composure, then slanted her a glance. "I've never known anybody who could catch a fish without getting out of his bedroll."

She blinked. "Huh?"

"Come on. Break out that rain gear you're so proud of. I can hear the lake trout calling this morning. There's a lunker out there with my name on it."

"If you catch it, I'll cook it," she offered.

He gave her a thumbs-up in agreement. "You're on."

Two hours later, Cassie had landed a string of three modest trout. Michael had been skunked.

"Beginner's luck," he grumbled, carrying the cooked fish inside the tent.

He found Cassie sitting cross-legged on her bedroll. He was immediately curious about her silence when he noticed she was watching the mink's explorations of his new surroundings. The little guy hobbled around on three legs, stopping now and then to gnaw on his bandage.

Cassie looked up and smiled as Michael hunched down opposite her. He held her gaze, thinking that looking into her blue eyes for an eternity wouldn't be enough time, and two seconds was much too long. He'd better hope the rain ended soon. An entire day cooped up with her in this tent and he'd be a basket case for sure.

Looking smug, she used a fork to slide one of the fish from the frying pan onto her plate. "The secret of catching fish must be to have a lucky guide," she said, a mischievous sparkle in her eyes. "One who knows right where to find them."

"And a guide who is too dumb to catch one himself." He pulled the hood of his rain jacket back. "Double or nothing next time."

"Be careful. You might lose again."

"To a rank amateur? Impossible."

"We'll see. It may take me a while to catch on to somethin' new, but once I do, I'm a whiz." She grinned at him impishly then broke off a bite of fish, offering it to Ernie. The mink approached her cautiously, sniffed the tips of her fingers, and nervously backed away again. "Come on, baby cakes. Michael made you a yummy breakfast with the fish *I* caught."

"You don't have to rub it in."

"I want Ernie to appreciate your efforts."

His lips twitched. "Yeah. Sure you do."

Screwing up his courage, the mink ate the offered morsel, then slowly licked Cassie's fingertips.

"I don't know how you can get a wild animal to act so tame," Michael said. "If I tried that, he'd bite my hand off."

"It's easy. I had a goldfish when I was kid. You know, the kind you win at the school carnival by tossing rings? Anyway, he was real cute with a big white spot on his side and a funny pug nose. I called him Porkie, and he used to eat out of my hand and then I'd pet him."

He looked at her incredulously. Nobody had a performing goldfish. Except Cassie.

TO THE ACCOMPANIMENT of a steady rainfall, they played gin rummy for the rest of the morning and on into the afternoon. Michael intentionally stopped keeping score when Cassie reached ten thousand points. He considered suggesting they switch to a more interesting game, like strip poker, but figured he'd get damn cold with no clothes on.

He usually had better luck at cards... and fishing. Clearly, Cassie was the kind of distraction a serious guy could do without.

At last the sun broke through the clouds.

When Cassie crawled out of the tent, she felt like a butterfly finally released from its cocoon into a world filled with fresh air and eye-squinting light. The firs and pines were a vibrant green, their needles washed sparkling clean by raindrops. Fingertips tucked into her hip pockets, she strolled down to the shore with Michael, wishing in that secret place in her heart that she could hold his hand. Ernie hobbled along behind them trying to keep up.

"This is so wonderful," she said on a sigh. The remaining dark clouds were edged in silver, and columns of light streamed through the breaks between them. On the lake, the water undulated with tiny whitecaps the brisk breeze lifted and spirited across the surface. Birds that had taken shelter during the storm were busily searching for food, darting this way and that along the shore.

She watched as Michael righted their carefully beached canoe and checked the gear. His movements were agile, heart-stoppingly masculine.

Cassie drew a deep, longing breath, and blew out a sigh. "Have you always lived in northern Minnesota?" she asked, so curious about him she risked another question about his past.

"Yeah. I was born in Ely. My dad and I moved to Gunflint after my mother passed away. I was ten."

"That's a hard age to lose a mother."

He spread out the map on a large, flat boulder next to the lake and laid his compass on top of it. "I don't suppose there's any good time to have a parent die." With the back of his hand, he shooed Ernie away from where he was working. The mink hissed, then retreated.

"I don't remember my folks."

Sitting back on his haunches, Michael looked up at her, his forehead furrowed by a pair of wavy lines. "I'm sorry."

"It's no big deal. Sure, I wish I'd had real parents, but since they went off and left me, I figure I was better off with my Aunt Myrtle. We got along real good." She shifted her gaze to watch the graceful flight of an eagle. "Then she got sick. Alzheimer's, they said. So I decided it was my turn to take care of her. I dropped out of school when I was fifteen and went to work full time. I kept her at home as long as I could."

"But you were just a kid. How could you manage?"

"She wasn't too bad at first. Kinda' forgetful is all, so she lost her job, not that it had been all that great shakes of a job, anyway."

"That's a helluva responsibility for anyone, much less a teenager."

"Not really." Cassie would have willingly done it all over again to have her aunt back. There'd been so many happy times, the bad years didn't count.

"You must have loved each other very much."

Cassie turned, planning to agree with his statement, but instead she screeched, "Ernie! Leave Michael's things alone!" She lunged for the compass the mink had batted to the edge of the rock.

Too late.

The compass plunked into the lake. For a moment it remained visible as it sank through the clear water. Then it dropped out of sight.

Michael roared like a wounded bear. "I'm gonna kill him. I swear I am."

Cassie winced. "He didn't mean any harm."

With a lopsided gait, Ernie fled the scene.

"Don't worry. I'll get the compass," Cassie announced. Sitting in order to take her shoes off, she'd worked one bootlace loose when Michael grabbed her arm and hauled her unceremoniously to her feet.

"Do you have any idea how deep the water is here? Or how cold?"

"Well, no, but it can't be—"

"There's a twenty- or thirty-foot vertical drop to a muddy bottom. And the water temperature below the top two or three feet is rarely above fifty degrees. Just how long do you think you can hold your breath, Ms. Seeger? Assuming you could possibly overcome the hypothermia that's sure to follow a dip in the lake, much less find the damn compass once you got down to all that silt."

"I could try." Her chin wobbled. She didn't like the way his lips were drawn into a grim line or the narrowed look of his eyes.

"And probably drown yourself in the process." He manhandled her back up the shore toward their campsite. "The good news is, this means this whole trip is off. We're going back home tomorrow."

"Now wait just one darn minute!" Digging in her heels, she shrugged away from his grasp. "We've come this far. I'm not going to quit now. And I won't let you quit, either."

"You don't have any choice. Without a compass we don't have one chance in ten thousand of finding that damn little white spot on the map."

"Sure we do." She didn't want to let go of her dream. Making plans for the future had kept Cassie going when things had gotten really rough, like the miserable day she'd finally decided she could no longer take care of her aunt. At the convalescent hospital she and Myrtle had talked of nothing else, only of her dreams and making them come true. Eventually Aunt Myrtle had forgotten about Way Quah, or even who she was, but Cassie had kept on talking. And dreaming.

After Aunt Myrtle passed on, Cassie had poured all of her love into the lives of her regulars at the coffee shop. For them she had to carry on, to help Flossie and Jack and Eldyne and Ernie, and all the other lonely folks who needed a boost up the ladder of happiness.

Besides, Cassie didn't want to give up one extra moment she might spend with Michael, in spite of the fact he could be a real pain in the butt. Men were like that, she decided. At least men who were worth their salt. Besides, she figured in some strange way he needed her, like the troubled Vietnam vet who needed a little extra caring to go with his hash browns.

"The sun and stars have been around a lot longer than compasses," she pointed out. "You can navigate that way. And if we get lost, who cares? All we have to do is head south. We'll pop out in civilization someplace."

"You want me to navigate by dead reckoning?"

She gave him her brightest, albeit forced, smile. "I'm sure you'll do just fine. You're a wonderful guide. Everyone I asked said so. We'll get to Way Quah in no time at all."

He threw up his arms in exasperation. Cassie was the most stubborn, bullheaded, never-say-die... He didn't deserve that kind of blind trust. No one did. Particularly a guy like him who had put another woman at risk. Unnecessarily. And, God help him, destroyed their son in the process.

He lowered his gaze and glowered at Cassie. "How much do you really know about Way Quah?" he asked. A muscle rippled in his jaw.

"I know that finding Way Quah means you've found the secret of happiness."

"That's the biggest lie of all. What other nonsense have you heard?"

She lifted her shoulders slightly. "I didn't just hear it. I read about the enchanted village in an old trapper's diary. He ought to know."

"Because it was written down, you believed it?"

"Of course."

"Had he actually been to Way Quah?"

"Well, no," she admitted, folding her arms across her chest. "But he had a friend who'd told him all about it."

"Did you find *any* eyewitness accounts?" he persisted.

"Not exactly. There are all sorts of Indian legends, though. Each one of them is a little bit different, but you know that. The village is out there somewhere. I'm sure it is."

He took a step toward her—a threatening step. "Then I can assume you know about the Dream Catchers?"

"Well, sort of." She backed away. "There was a mention of something like that in one of the books I read. But no details."

"They're guardians of Way Quah, Cassie. If they exist at all—and as far as I'm concerned they are as much a myth as the enchanted village itself—the Dream Catchers don't let just anybody into town." The memory of the storyteller's drumbeat throbbed in his head. With adolescent arrogance, he had only thought of the physical challenge the quest offered. He had no fear of the supernatural. He still refused to acknowledge that possibility. "They're a very protective lot."

"But if we go there, to that little place on the map, how can they keep us out?"

"Before you can reach Way Quah, again assuming it exists, you have to pass a series of tests." For him it had been hunger, terrible thirst and physical exhaustion. The memories were vague now, and only the sting of broken promises remained. He'd found no secret formula to assure happiness. "According to legend, they're very difficult tests."

She scowled. "I wasn't all that good in school."

He blew out a breath. "This doesn't have anything to do with academic work. In this case, you'll have to prove you're strong." According to the stories he'd heard told around a camp fire, some mythical travelers had to fight wolverines, the fiercest animal his ancestors knew.

She puffed out her chest as if to show courage, which managed to raise her breasts in a very enticing way. Michael wondered how such a simple action could break through his memories to heat his blood and make him think about an entirely different subject.

"I carried your darn canoe, didn't I?" she reminded him. "And climbed up that stupid cliff of yours, in spite of the fact I was scared spitless."

"Well, yeah. I'm sorry about both of those things. But you're missing the point." Or maybe *he* was, because he was beginning to find the petulant shape of her lips quite inviting. "This particular test has to do with being strong on the inside, not just muscle power."

Lifting her chin stubbornly, she said, "I'm tough. Ask anyone. I can take a whole lot of guff from customers before I lose my cool. That ought to count for something."

She'd taken a lot of static from him, he realized. And he wasn't done yet. "You'll also have to pass a test for bravery, and you'll recall that you didn't do real well with the timber wolf last night."

"He startled me, that's all. Besides, he was spooky. And don't tell me I have to wrestle a wolf in order to qualify for a tourist visa to Way Quah. I never read anything about that at the library."

Why hadn't some guy taken this woman in hand and taught her more productive activities than spending the day at the library? Activities like making love on satin sheets, like being kissed senseless, like letting a man bury himself within her soft, warm flesh. "I don't think you'll have any trouble with the test of compassion." He looked pointedly at Ernie, who was cowering in a patch of grass. "Wisdom might be another story." He wouldn't relate the tests of love and trust the storyteller had mentioned. Those had not been a part of his quest, though perhaps he had been too young. Likely those would be the easy challenges for a woman like Cassie, anyway.

"Ah, come on. You're making this whole thing up because you want me to quit."

"I want you to know what you're getting into. *If* we decide to keep going, and *if* the legends are true—which are both very big question marks at this point—we could be in for considerable trouble."

"Well, if we don't keep trying then we'll fail for sure, and that would be like not trying at all. My Aunt Myrtle always said—"

"Your Aunt Myrtle didn't have to face the Old Man of the Forest."

"Who's he?" she asked blankly.

"An evil spirit that blocks the path to Way Quah."

"Some ol' friend of the guardians, I suppose." She gave a dismissive wave of her hand.

"No. That's what makes him so dangerous, according to the story." The memory of a bitterly cold day washed over him, making Michael shiver. "The Old Man is their enemy, too. He can take many forms. A blizzard—"

"In August? I'm not exactly worried about that."

"A wolverine," he continued. "A crazed bear. An unexplained illness. There's no way of knowing."

"For somebody who doesn't believe in Way Quah, you sure know a lot of about it," she pointed out with a wry twist of her lips.

"When I was a boy I listened to the storytellers around my grandfather's camp fire. Their tales were frightening." A shudder ran down his spine at the memory. Perhaps the old storyteller had been wise to warn against any attempt to visit the enchanted village, a warning he had once ignored.

"Michael Longlake, you're making fun of me just to scare me off. I figure I can be as strong and brave as anybody else. Pound for pound, I mean. And I'm not afraid of some cranky old man, whatever he looks like. I admit you'll have to handle the wisdom part."

Michael wasn't so sure he could. He was about to do something very foolish. Maybe it was the stubborn way Cassie faced him down. Or the capacity for love she had demonstrated more than once, which he had lost somewhere along the way. Or more likely it was the contour of her lips, her sweet scent and the memory of how she'd felt, naked and pliable, in his arms.

He didn't want to fall into that trap again, the jaws that closed painfully around a man when he needed a woman so much and then she was gone. But he felt the pull of that power so keenly he could no longer resist.

Cupping her chin, he rasped his thumb across her pouty lower lip.

"What makes you so darn stubborn, Cassie Seeger?"

Her lip trembled. "Just made that way, I guess."

Slowly, he lowered his head. She might not know it, but she was made for kissing and tasting, and for being held during long winter nights.

Chapter Seven

Cassie watched with trembling anticipation as Michael's head dipped toward hers. His long, tapered fingers held her in a gentle vise, one she had no desire to escape. His fresh breath softly caressed her cheeks, and she inhaled deeply of his masculine scent.

The first touch of his lips sent warmth curling through her body. Her heart rate accelerated. In her mind, images splintered like the brightest flare of northern lights, colors arching across the sky, dragging a sigh of wonder from her throat. She rested her hand on his wrist to steady herself, or maybe because she needed to strengthen the connection between them beyond the tentative joining of their lips.

In the silence of the woods, she heard the breeze shifting through the pine branches, and the muted lap of wavelets brushing against the shore. The sounds pressed in on her awareness, cocooning her, focusing her entire attention on Michael's kiss and the electrifying sensation it produced. Her pulse quickened yet again.

She was kissing Michael. How long had she waited for this moment? *A lifetime.*

Michael shifted his head, crossing her mouth again, skimming his tongue along the seam of her lips. Her sweet flavor drugged his reason. Hunger clawed at him. And need. The ravenous need of a starving man who had been deprived for far too long.

He slid his tongue into her velvety warmth. Her low, throaty sound of welcome licked over his senses and tightened the aching muscles in his groin.

The power of his desire shocked him. He hadn't known he was still capable of such urgent need. And he couldn't let this happen. Not with Cassie. It wasn't fair. To her. Or him. His feelings were only illusory, like the enchanted village she sought. His job was to guide her to nowhere and then safely home again. He dared not give in to the primitive urges she stirred within him.

Steeling himself for the ultimate sacrifice of denial, he raised his head. Her eyes fluttered open. Irises dark with passion questioned him.

He cursed his foolhardy nobility. "This is no good, Cassie."

"I thought..." Her voice caught. "I thought it was pretty nice."

"I only mean we can't...I'm supposed to be your guide. Kissing you is...unprofessional."

She lifted her chin. "Sorry. I didn't know there was a north-woods code of ethics against a friendly peck or two. Maybe," she said tartly, visibly drawing on some inner strength, "after we see Way Quah and get back home again, you'll show me a copy of the code. It ought to be at least as interesting to read as the back of a cereal box."

His lips twitched. The woman bounced back so fast it made his head spin. And made him wonder if he had been the only one to experience the power of the kiss they had shared. *Friendly peck?* Hell, that was the sexiest kiss he'd ever known.

"WE WILL HAVE TO WARN them away."

"You have already tried to frighten her and still they persist."

"There are other ways. The man will recognize the signals."

"I think he is already blinded and does not yet know it."

"This time he will heed me. If not, he will have to face the Old Man of the Forest."

She shuddered. She sensed the woman was too strong and the man had too much courage to fail.

For their sake, she would have to watch. Perhaps there would be a way she could help them on their journey.

She smiled to herself. Gray Wolf would not be pleased with her decision.

Nor would the Old Man, she realized, resting her hand protectively on her swollen belly.

In that moment, she realized to distract Gray Wolf's attention from the travelers she would have to ask her mate Night Hawk for help.

BEFORE DAWN THE NEXT morning, Michael slipped quietly out of the tent. He told himself it was because he wanted to be on the lake at first light to catch a few fish for breakfast. Alone.

Truth was, he hadn't slept worth a damn. He thought Cassie had been restless, too. Every time she turned or made the slightest sound, he heard her. And wanted her. He couldn't keep his thoughts away from the taste of her lips, or the silken curves of her body. And when he did manage to sleep, her image invaded his dreams.

He jammed the paddle hard into the water and stroked with as much force as he could. Maybe a little exercise would help him get Cassie out of his mind.

He went the length of the lake where they had camped and turned into a secluded bay. Morning mist still clung to the treetops in wispy tendrils. When a beaver dam blocked his route, he pulled on his thigh-high waders, climbed out of the canoe and lifted it over the barrier.

The narrow lane he found was flooded, thanks to the beavers' efforts. Greenstone lava flows rose up to cliffs topped with pine. In boggy areas, blue irises the color of Cassie's eyes stood straight and tall, well rooted against nature's forces just like the woman he knew.

Letting the canoe's momentum carry him past the scenery, he wished he had waited for Cassie to wake up. She would have liked this quiet, still place. And her melodic voice would have chased away the feeling of loneliness that hovered here, like the mist crowding down on the treetops.

Ah, Cassie. Why couldn't you have tried for Atlantis, instead?

Turning, he stroked the boat back the way he had come. On the air currents that wafted through the tops of the trees he caught an unusual scent, something rotting and putrid.

Then he saw it.

Within the brief moments he'd been in the narrow valley, someone had stripped two birch saplings of every branch and bent them nearly to the breaking point, crossing them above the beaver dam. An object dangled from the middle. At first Michael thought it was a flag of some sort. But as he drew closer he realized the fabric was stuffed with grass, like an oversize doll his ancestors had made for their children. Stick arms had been added and the whole thing was trussed up with a woven reed rope twisted around what should have been the throat.

Fear snaked through Michael's gut.

The doll, if that's what you could call it, had been stuffed into Cassie's powder blue T-shirt. The one with the slogan Way Quah Or Bust.

Not bothering with waders, Michael leapt out of the canoe. He grabbed hold of the doll... and Cassie's shirt... tugging it lower until he could reach the rope. He used his hunting knife to cut the obscene warning free, then tossed the whole thing into the canoe.

Released, the trees whipped upright again.

Frantically, he scanned the narrow valley between the greenstone cliffs, and then checked what he could see of the top. How could they have known where he was going? How could they have acted so quickly? And who... who could be warning them away? He didn't even wish to consider why the air now carried the pungent scent of putrefaction, an unforgettable odor he recalled from his youthful vision quest. He didn't dare fully explore the implications of that dark memory.

"Leave her alone!" he bellowed. "She doesn't mean you any harm."

His shout raised a flock of blackbirds that squawked angrily as they rose into the air.

He lifted the canoe back over the beaver dam, breaking away sections of sticks and leaves in his hurry. Water spilled over the top. This was only a warning, he told himself. No harm had come to Cassie yet. He'd see to it none did.

CASSIE PICKED UP a flat stone and skipped it across the placid lake. Five bounces. Not bad for someone who was so mad she could spit tacks.

She slanted Ernie a glance. "You really should learn to behave yourself around Michael, baby cakes. It's not nice to make him mad. But you don't have to worry about him killing you. He just needed to huff and puff a bit. Men do that sometimes when they're upset. Not that being grouchy is limited to men, you understand. Sometimes when Flossie comes into the coffee shop she's got a chip on her shoulder so big even Paul Bunyon would be afraid to knock it off."

Ignoring Cassie's one-sided conversation, the mink continued to sun himself on a boulder, not in the least interested in Flossie's problems, or concerned about Michael's moods or his absence.

Cassie was. He shouldn't have gone off and left her alone. If he wanted to be the one to catch their breakfast, she would have let him. She wouldn't have even put her line in the water, if that's what he wanted. A stupid fish didn't mean that much to her.

And it wasn't her fault she'd *liked* Michael's kiss. A whole lot. It's not as if a woman could turn her feelings on and off willy-nilly. It didn't necessarily mean she was going to jump the guy just because he had the warmest, most sensuous lips she'd ever known. Though admittedly she might have given the idea a little more thought if he'd shown the least bit of interest.

Which he hadn't.

So she was all alone. Except for a lame mink. And she was suddenly more lonely than she had ever been in her entire life.

Dragging out a sigh, she folded her arms across her chest and rubbed the morning chill from her upper arms. He'd come back soon, she told herself.

A movement in the dark shadows on the opposite shore caught her eye. A graceful doe edged out of the pine forest, glanced warily from side to side, then lowered her head to drink. When she looked up again, her gaze seemed to settle on Cassie.

Cassie remained motionless. "Hi, pretty lady," she whispered. "Wish I had my camera with me." Although, because of a high cloud cover, she doubted there'd be enough light for a really sharp photo at this distance. It was just as well. She'd been snapping pictures at a much faster rate than she had anticipated and didn't have all that much film left. She had to save at least a roll to record Way Quah. Her friends at the coffee shop would be anxious to see what she discovered.

Ernie wasn't very interested in keeping quiet. He made a sound that was a lot like a bark.

The doe lifted her head. Her nostrils flared and her ears stood rigidly at attention. She twitched her tail.

As though he'd been scolded, Ernie scurried with a lopsided gait off the boulder where he'd been perched and hid among the shrubbery.

"The mama deer won't hurt you, baby cakes," Cassie crooned with a soft chuckle. "She's clear on the other side of the lake."

A moment later, the deer vanished back into the woods and Cassie spotted Michael's canoe arrowing up the lake. The V-shaped wake of the shiny craft created a silver wave as he paddled toward her.

She had geared up to throw a rip-roaring, foot-stamping temper tantrum because he'd gone off without a word. Instead, she was simply too glad to see him to feel anything but relief.

Hopeless desire slid through her, and she felt her insides turn to warm jelly as she remembered the exquisite heat of his kiss. Darn it all! She was falling head over teakettle for a guy who talked about professional ethics!

"So, how many fish did you catch?" she asked as he levered himself out of the boat. "I suppose you thought going off alone was the only way you'd win the bet and I'd have to do the cooking."

Michael pulled the canoe out of the water. Breakfast was the last thing on his mind. "No fish. I didn't even get my line wet."

She frowned. "But that's why I thought you went off—"

"I found this, Cassie." He held up the bundle of grass and sticks.

"You found my T-shirt! I wondered where that had got to. I was looking all over the place this morning. Arletta and the others would have been real disappointed if I'd lost it. They took up a collection, you know. I thought it was so sweet of 'em. She's always doing nice things like—"

"Cassie! I didn't just find your shirt. It was left for me. As a warning."

She stared incredulously at the shirt and then back at him. The lingering scent of rotten eggs tickled her nostrils, and a shiver raised gooseflesh on her arms. "Warning? What on earth for?"

"Because someone doesn't want us messing around up here."

"Nonsense. Why would anyone give a fig about us looking for Way Quah? It's a free country."

"Maybe the warning doesn't have anything to do with your mythical enchanted village." He jammed his hands into his pockets, knowing he couldn't bring himself to voice any fanciful explanations that would satisfy Cassie's active imagination. "Maybe, just maybe, it has to do with smuggling."

As she weighed that possibility, a cute little frown pleated her forehead. "Smuggling? Here? Why, there's nothing around except pinecones."

"This is border country, Cassie. Things go back and forth across lines. Illegal things. Like drugs. And untaxed booze." The explanation was about as rational as he could make it. The facts might even fit. He almost hoped it was true.

She shook her head. "Well, smuggling is no concern of ours. Naturally, I don't approve of that sort of thing, but that doesn't mean we're here trying to play cops and robbers. That's got to be obvious. I'm sure if we leave them alone, they won't bother us."

He massaged the bridge of his nose with his fingertips. He had the terrible feeling she wasn't going to quit, no matter what he said. "That's not always how it works, Cassie. If we have stumbled onto some kind of a smuggling ring, they may not believe in Way Quah any more than I do. And they might not give you a chance to explain your nice little map before the both of us simply vanish off the face of the earth . . . drowned at the bottom of some lake."

"Oh . . ." she said thoughtfully. "Then you know for sure smuggling goes on here? They've caught people in the act?"

The only thing he knew for sure was that he had an eerie feeling he didn't like, an anxious feeling that burrowed like a tick under his skin and then itched like crazy. "Canadians get caught once in a while buying stuff in Grand Marais and trying to sneak it back over the border without paying duty. Taxes are real high up north."

"That hardly sounds like big-time smuggling activity. What about drugs?"

"Kids occasionally try to bring some in over the border. In their car trunks. That kind of thing."

"But at regular border crossings?"

"Well, yeah," he admitted. "Most of the time."

She hooked the back of her wrist at the curve of her hip and lifted her haughty little chin. "You may think it was smugglers who made off with my shirt, in spite of the fact we haven't seen hide nor hair of anyone since the first day we were out on the lakes. But I've got another theory."

He was definitely afraid to ask. "What's that?"

"The guardians."

He swallowed hard the words of denial. "Who?"

"The Dream Catchers you told me about. The folks who are in charge of protecting the enchanted village. I'll just bet this is one of their tests. Courage, or something."

With a quick shake of his head, he fought off another fleeting image of his adolescent vision quest. "No, Cassie, the Dream Catchers aren't real. They're only a fantasy."

"So are your dumb smugglers. You're just trying to frighten me."

Damn her! She was the most stubborn, determined... He wanted to wrap his fingers around her throat, that tempting slender column, and... and... kiss her senseless. That's what he wanted to do. He wouldn't, of course. What he had to do was get them out of here and away from whoever... or whatever... had placed that warning doll in his path.

"Get your things packed," he ordered. "We're leaving for home."

"Home? You promised to take me to Way Quah."

"I told you, without the compass we'll be lucky to get back to where we started. And I'm not going to risk our necks for something that doesn't exist, particularly with God knows who out there trying to warn us away." Hoping she wouldn't argue with him further, he lowered his voice to a threatening level. "You got that?"

She started to say something then gave it up. "What about breakfast?"

"We'll have a couple of granola bars. Or you can have a Twinkie."

"I already ate the last two this morning," she grumbled as she turned and stalked away.

THERE SHOULDN'T BE RAPIDS here...no white water for miles. At least that was what Michael thought as he struggled to keep the canoe in the middle of the raging stream swollen by the recent rains. How the hell had he gotten so far off track? Distracted by the building cloud cover, he'd managed to get his directions all screwed up. Clearly he'd missed a turn that should have taken them back to Gunflint Lake. Or at the very least he'd found a very dangerous alternate route.

He'd figure it out later. Right now he had to keep the canoe from breaking apart on the granite boulders strewn in its path.

The boat dipped and twisted, then the next instant rode up another wave only to drop with a jolt through a watery crevasse. Spray rose like a tidal surge and swept past the canoe in a mass of curling foam.

Michael swallowed enough water to float a steamer. He coughed and swiped away the water from his eyes.

"Hang on, Cassie!" he shouted.

"This is great!" she called back to him, water pouring over her head. She swung her paddle from side to side, ineffectually trying to shove them away from the danger of one boulder only to realize that particular peril had been replaced by a new one.

With a twist of his paddle, Michael slewed the boat over a three-foot drop. This kind of white water was made for hotdogging, he thought, not for an amateur like Cassie. She should at least have a helmet on. If they capsized she'd bash her head on the rocks. So would he, for that matter. He'd never expected to get them into this kind of mess, and wondered what malevolent force had led them here.

The current yanked and pulled at the boat. More than once the canoe slid through the water sideways, then turned and sent its stern downstream. Michael righted them again, paddling for all he was worth. Without the sheen of water on his face, he knew he'd be sweating. His shoulder sockets burned with his effort. His lungs labored to keep up with the demands the river placed on him.

The rapids seemed endless. He couldn't remember anything on the map, or within his experience, that would have warned him of the danger. They were being catapulted through a narrow rift that didn't exist.

A crease in time, his grandfather would have called it.

Impossible.

But it was here. And potentially deadly.

A wave of foam lifted them. The canoe broached, slid down a trough and teetered on the brink of capsizing.

Michael threw his weight the opposite direction. His paddle slammed into a crack between rocks he hadn't noticed. With enormous force, the boulders snatched the paddle from his grasp as the current whipped the canoe downstream.

He fought a rising tide of panic. Without a paddle he didn't have a prayer of keeping the canoe upright, much less in the safest part of the stream. Neither did the inexperienced Cassie. And there was no way to get the paddle from her with her sitting ten feet from him in the bow, not with the boat rocking and tipping through the churning river.

Spying a particularly wild section of water up ahead, he shouted, "Paddle left!"

"Okay," her voice sang out.

Her oar made it into the water about one out of four tries, stroking through the air the rest of the time. Yet miraculously the canoe veered the direction Michael had hoped. They shot past the dangerous spot like a rocket.

"Now, right!" he ordered.

The roar of the tumbling water drowned her reply but she did as he asked. He had little hope she could maneuver them through the tight turn coming up. Neither her strength nor her finesse with the paddle would be enough. Bracing himself, he waited for the bone-jarring impact of the canoe against granite.

The bow dipped and rocked. Cassie wielded her paddle like a magic wand. Michael watched with growing amazement as they zigzagged almost effortlessly past giant boulders, down a waterfall—that from this perspective rivaled Niagara—then exploded out of the chute into the calm waters of a lake. To his amazement, he heard Cassie yodeling— as if she was on a sporty weekend outing for heaven's sake. Had she no idea of the danger they had just escaped?

Shaking his head, he felt a laugh born of relief vibrate through his chest. None of this was real. Their boat and all of the contents, including little Ernie, should have been strewn from one end of the white water to the other. He and Cassie should have been battered and bloodied, if not smashed to bits. Yet there she sat, pretty as you please, singing. The woman was incredible!

He leaned back and released the pent-up laughter that had been building...maybe for years. He roared. He simply couldn't help himself.

Cassie heard the unfamiliar sound. Startled, she swiveled her head. Already filled with adrenaline from the wild ride, her heart revved up an additional notch at the sight of Michael laughing. One side of his mouth curled higher than the other, and a devastatingly attractive dimple creased his cheek. The corners of his eyes crinkled with amusement. Lord, her heart felt as if it would burst with happiness, and she knew she was a goner for sure.

Helplessly, she grinned back at him. "Was that great, or what? Better than any roller coaster I've ever ridden."

He ran the back of his hand across his mouth, as though trying to disguise the fact he was capable of such a dazzling smile.

"Cassie, would you mind paddling us to shore? There's a nice little beach over there." His chuckle was low and throaty and totally sexy as he pointed off to her right. "I think we could both use a breather."

"Sure. No problem." Though she wondered why he didn't head them that direction himself. She glanced around and saw him sitting at the back of the boat, hands empty. Her eyes widened.

"Michael, where's your paddle?"

"I dropped it. About halfway through the rapids."

"Why'd you do that?" Frowning, she looked at him incredulously. "You know I don't have any idea how to steer this thing."

Running his fingers through his wet hair to comb the lank strands away from his forehead, he said, "Trust me. I didn't intend to lose the paddle. The river, however, had a different idea."

Her jaw went slack and she felt the blood drain from her face. If she'd been standing, she knew her legs would have gone rubbery, her knees weak. "You mean all that time...I was the only one..." The reality of their situation nearly overwhelmed her. "My God, Michael, we could have been killed!" she wailed.

"I know. Incredible, isn't it?"

"But I wasn't even scared." Though if she'd known the facts she would have been terrified. "I thought you had everything under control."

"Not likely."

A wave of dizziness threatened. "Here, you take this," she said, offering him their one remaining paddle with shaking hands. "I'd be too afraid I'd drop this one and then we'd really be stuck."

He grinned at her, a sweet smile that sent a curl of warmth right to her midsection. "We're okay now. Or we will be once we get dried off." He dipped the paddle into the water and stroked for shore, adding ominously, "And when I figure out where the hell we are."

Chapter Eight

An unusually cool breeze riffled the water as Michael eased the canoe toward the beach. Dark clouds billowed in the distance. He rasped the bow skid plate up onto the sand, hopped out and trudged through the water to drag the boat onto dry land. It was a miracle they were all still in one piece.

He was hefting a portage pack out of the canoe when he realized Cassie hadn't moved, not so much as a twitch since she'd given him the paddle. She was still sitting at the bow of the boat, a silly, sexy little grin quirking her lips as her eyes followed his every movement.

"Out you go," he ordered. "We took on a lot of water. Let's get it bailed out."

"I'm not real sure I can move."

He cast her a worried look. "Are you hurt?"

"No," she replied in an odd, soft voice. "I don't

think so. A bruise or two. Mostly my legs are feeling real weak. Kinda rubbery.''

"It's the excitement." He was suffering from the same ailment. His heart was pounding a bit too fast, his breathing rapid and shallow. Looking at Cassie did nothing to take the edge off his adrenaline high.

He cupped her elbow to help her out of the boat.

She stood a little unsteadily. Her eyes were wide with wonder as she palmed his cheek, her gentle fingers softly caressing him. Her wet T-shirt clung to her, emphasizing the soft curves of her body and revealing hardened nipples puckered beneath the fabric. Michael stifled a groan.

Instinctively, his hands sought the tapered shape of her midriff to steady her, his thumbs managing to skim the swell of her breasts in the process. He lifted her from the canoe. Light as a feather. Delicate. Desirable.

She rocked against him. The muscles of his groin tightened.

"Michael, do you realize what we just did?"

He was much more aware of what he *wanted* to do. Right now. Here on the beach. Valiantly, he tried to suppress the thoughts that assailed him, and the image of Cassie naked and yielding in his arms.

Clearing his throat, he said, "We ran the wildest bit of white water I've ever seen."

"More than that. We passed one of their tests."

"What are you talking about?" Granted, his self-control was certainly being tested at this particular moment, but he didn't think Cassie would realize that. Unless he pulled her closer. Then she'd get the idea.

"The Dream Catchers. They were testing us. Courage or strength. Maybe both." She looked up at him with such naive confidence he could almost believe what she said was true. "And we passed! That means we must be getting very near Way Quah."

A band of anxiety tightened around his chest. It couldn't be... "Cassie, our survival in the rapids had nothing to do with courage or strength. It was sheer, blind luck. Nothing more."

"You're wrong."

"How can you say that?" Unable to stop himself, he wrapped his arms around her, held her close and rested his cheek against her damp, sweet-smelling hair. He refused to think about the consequences if she was right. "You hardly knew about the Dream Catchers and their tests until I told you that part of the legend. What makes you so sure now that it's true?" He pressed a soft kiss to her forehead. So sweet.

She trembled. "Because I know you wouldn't lie to me."

"Not lie, Cassie. It's a myth. The whole thing is make-believe." He wanted to make-believe there was no past, no future, no lingering guilt that rested heavily on his shoulders and woke him in the night. He wanted to deny the reality that he should have been able to save two lives, and failed. He longed for the here and now, with this desirable woman in his arms. He ached to wake to her quirky smile every morning, to hear her bubbly chatter, peppered with sentences she didn't quite manage to finish before she bounded into another subject.

But he was locked into a truth that was shadowed by his past.

"You'll see," she insisted in a sultry whisper. "Soon, you'll be able to see."

He didn't think that was possible.

With a determined effort, Michael stepped away. He didn't want to get sucked into her fantasy. Coming back to reality was far too difficult. More than most, he knew when you cared, dreams could turn into nightmares. "I'm going to have to find high ground. Maybe I can spot a familiar ridge, or another landmark. That way we can tell where we are." He picked up a day pack that included their maps and slung it over his arm. "I should be back in an hour or so."

"Hey, wait a minute," she protested, grabbing his arm. "You're not going to leave me here all alone."

Glancing at the gray clouds scudding across the sky, he said, "You'll be fine. Just stick by the gear."

"Not on your life, Michael Longlake. We're in this thing together."

"The forest is pretty thick. It'll be rough going. You'll slow me down."

"I haven't yet, have I?"

No, he silently admitted. She'd taken to the rigors of back-country travel like a native. But at the moment he thought a little time alone would do them both good. He, at least, needed to cool off before he did something really stupid. Like kiss her again. And let nature take its course. Which it would, given half a chance.

His gaze slid to Ernie, who was still huddling in the canoe. Amazingly, he hadn't been tossed from the craft during their wild ride down the rapids. The pesky little guy was just the excuse Michael needed.

"You don't want to leave the mink alone, do you? It might not be safe," he warned. "There could be predators around."

Cassie slanted the little animal a troubled glance, then nailed Michael with one of her stubborn looks. "Oh, no, you don't, buster. I know what you're trying to do, and you can't get rid of me that easily. We'll just turn the canoe over and put Ernie's bed underneath. He'll be as safe as a caterpillar at a convention of butterflies."

Michael lifted an eyebrow and blew out a sigh. He knew better than to argue with Cassie when she got that determined look. She was the most intractable creature he'd ever met this side of a pack animal, and a hell of a lot prettier. Even now, after her thorough dousing by the white water, simply looking at her caused an urgent hunger to build within him. He could do little else than surrender to her demands.

Within a few minutes, they'd piled their gear on the beach and settled Ernie with a good supply of food in his temporary home under the upside-down canoe. Then they headed inland along a narrow deer trail, the pine forest so thick only a few rays of cloudy sunlight penetrated through to the undergrowth. Ferns grew everywhere. And flowers. Delicate blossoms raised their trumpeting heads toward the sun to catch the drops of rain and mist that nourished them. The air was filled with the rich scent of a damp earth.

Cassie snapped a hurried picture. She figured this was as good as it got. Beyond the next tree they passed, or the one after that, she fully expected to catch a glimpse of the enchanted village. She felt that close. And even closer to being in love.

She'd never experienced anything like the feelings she had for Michael. True, she hadn't known him all that long. And granted, there were times when he was a real grouch.

But without even trying, he touched something basic within her. It wasn't simply sex. She felt a connection, as though Michael were the one thing her life had been missing all of these years. In some unfathomable way, he was her other half. She was absolutely sure of it.

Of course, he hadn't seen that particular truth yet, she thought with a sigh as she ducked under a pine branch that crossed the path. Men were a little slow in that regard, knowing what was good for them, or so she'd been told. It was simply a question of time before he'd catch on. She intended to do everything she could to hurry the process along. Her Aunt Myrtle had always told her, once you aim your sights on something, hang on like your life depended upon it.

She zeroed in on Michael's back. A nice, broad target. She'd figure out a way, she promised herself.

A stiff, cold breeze shifted the top branches of the pines, sending down a cascade of needles. Cassie shivered.

A moment later they came to a clearing.

"Oh . . ." she said on a disappointed sigh.

An old log cabin gray with moss stood where she'd expected to see her enchanted village. Though no smoke rose from the stovepipe chimney, the path to the front door was worn from frequent use. The cabin looked so completely a part of the clearing, there was something welcoming about the sturdy building.

"Watch it," Michael warned, placing a restraining hand on Cassie's arm before she could race out in front of him. He didn't like the looks of this. As far as he knew, no one lived in this remote area and there were no cabins around. And if there were local residents, they were probably here illegally.

"Well, whoever lives here can probably help us," Cassie announced with cheerful optimism.

"Unless it's the guys who left the warning earlier."

She gave him a teasing grin. "Your infamous pinecone smugglers? I can hardly wait to meet them."

"Cassie, will you be serious. If I'm right, we could be in danger." If the legend of the Dream Catchers was true, their situation could be even more perilous. But he couldn't believe that.

She looped her arm through his, giving him a quick squeeze that he felt echo in a hug around his heart. "I'm not afraid. Not when I'm with you."

No one should have that much trust in another person. It was dangerous and foolhardy. But Cassie wouldn't worry about that. One time, not so long ago, Michael had failed to live up to another woman's expectations.

From the shadow of the cabin a dark figure appeared. Huge. Moving silently on powerfully muscled legs.

Cassie drew an audible breath.

The bear lumbered toward them, his head shifting from side to side in a rhythmic motion. His nostrils flared. A low rumble vibrated from deep in his chest. The animal's thick fur had a chestnut hue, which Michael knew was a color variation of the native black bear. This was an unusually large specimen.

"Back up, Cassie," he ordered. "Nice and easy. Black bears are nearsighted. They don't usually attack people."

"That's reassuring," she said on a high-pitched squeak.

"Hi fella," he said loudly. "I wish I had a couple of cans I could clank together so you'd know we're people, not prey." He looped his arm around Cassie's slender waist, dragging her backward away from the bear. "Talk to him. Let him know who we are."

"You really think he's a good conversationalist?"

"Try." The bear kept stalking them as they retreated. His yellow eyes swept past them with each threatening arc of his thick neck. "If he attacks I want you to run as fast as you can, find a tree and climb it. You understand?"

"I'm not going to leave you alone."

In the hope of creating a defensive barrier, Michael worked them into a thicker part of the forest where trees grew only a few feet apart. Branches scraped across his back. "I'll distract him while you're getting away."

"Wonderful. Then what am I supposed to do? And what happens if the bear takes after me and decides he likes climbing trees?"

"He won't." That wasn't entirely out of the question, but Michael intended to keep the bear's attention while Cassie got safely away.

A clap of thunder rattled through the woods, followed by a quick sheet of lightning slicing across the sky. The air crackled with electricity and smelled of burned wood.

Michael felt Cassie shiver as the first drops of rain pelted the highest branches.

"It's okay," he whispered. He picked up a fallen branch from the forest floor and wrapped his fingers tightly around its thickness. Not a particularly good weapon, but he was more interested in making humanlike sounds rather than trying to defend himself with nothing more than a hunting knife.

Only a few feet away, the animal plodded after them, snapping twigs and branches with each step. "The bear will lose interest in us in a minute," Michael assured her.

"I hope so. I don't like this."

Neither did he. The recollection of another animal attack churned through his belly. Whether it had been a childhood nightmare, or something from real life, he simply couldn't be sure. He only knew he had to protect Cassie.

He took his eyes off the bear for an instant to glance around. A fallen birch lay against another tree at a forty-five-degree angle, a pathway to safety, the top of the log well out of reach for the muscular bear. *If* they could climb high enough, fast enough. And the bear didn't follow.

He shoved Cassie that direction. "Climb," he ordered, giving her a boost with his hand at her butt.

She scrambled onto the slanted trunk. "You're coming too, aren't you?"

"Right behind you."

But he'd run out of time.

Baring his age-yellowed fangs, the bear reared to his full height and roared. Another crash of thunder rattled across the landscape in chorus with the fierce growl. Dropping to all fours again, the animal broke into a run, a thousand pounds of fur heading directly for Michael.

Cassie screamed.

She smelled the creature as he ran beneath her precarious perch, a fetid odor that assailed her senses. Not like the wolf that had startled her at their campsite. Or the odor she'd detected on her climb up the cliff side. This was far more frightening because it tapped into a primitive part of her brain controlled by fear.

Unadulterated fear.

The sensation coiled tightly through her, mounting, a feeling so sharp it had weight and texture. *The Old Man of the Forest.*

The thought galvanized her energy. She fought back with all the courage she could muster. She had to protect Michael. Without him she knew reaching Way Quah would be meaningless. Unless she acted quickly he would be mauled to death.

Gathering splinters as she went, she slid down the tree. Michael's shouts echoed through the forest. She crashed through the woods along the trail the bear had broken in his crazed pursuit. Rain pelted her face. Or maybe they were fearful tears that blurred her vision.

She snatched up a broken limb from the ground. Slamming it against trees as she ran, she shouted, "Leave him alone, Old Man!"

She caught up with them at the edge of the lake. Michael had waded into the water and was waist deep in a sheltered cove. Cupping his hands, he sent splash after splash at the bear who was pacing along the shore. The animal snorted and tossed his head from side to side.

Picking up a handful of rocks, Cassie fired them at the animal's rump. "Go away!" she screamed.

"Cassie, get out of here," Michael ordered. "He'll turn on you."

"I know. It'll give you time to get away."

"You'll be killed."

Cassie didn't have time to worry about that. The bear had already turned in her direction. Sniffing the air, he moved deliberately toward her. Saliva dripped from his mouth. Menacing noises rumbled in his chest.

Her breath lodged painfully in her throat. Backing slowly away, she tried to force air into her heaving lungs. Oxygen starved, her legs grew weak. She was going to die and she hadn't yet had a chance to live . . . or love.

It wasn't fair. It simply wasn't fair that fear would have so much power over her.

Michael staggered back to shore. He pitched a rock at the bear and hit him square on the side of the head. "Run, Cassie!"

"I . . . can't."

Confused by two opponents, the bear snarled and looked in Michael's direction then back at Cassie.

"I'll distract him." Michael sent another barrage of stones at the bear. "Make for the cabin. You'll be safe there."

"If I leave, you might be killed."

Michael didn't like how the bear was very effectively herding Cassie toward the water. In a few more steps he'd have her cornered. In a swimming contest, the bear would be the winner. That had been Michael's own fear only minutes ago. "Cassie, for once in your life will you quit being so damn stubborn. Run!"

All of a sudden thunder cracked and lightning flashed. The earth shook as a nearby tree splintered and flared briefly before a renewed downpour doused the flames.

In the space that separated Cassie from the raging bear, a deer appeared. Michael didn't know how it had happened. He'd never heard of a doe challenging a larger animal, except perhaps to protect her young, which didn't seem to be the case now. But the deer was there. On the attack. Nostrils flaring, she scraped at the ground with her hoof. Angered or surprised, the bear slapped at her with his huge paw, only to have her hop easily out of his reach, almost as though she were goading him.

"Cassie, now's your chance. Get away while you can."

But the bear wasn't quite so easily distracted. He turned on Cassie again. She cried out in alarm.

Before the bear could make good on his new attack, the doe countered with three swift strokes of her hind legs to the bear's head. The larger animal bellowed in anger. He set his sights and lunged toward the doe. This time she bolted into the woods, the bear close on her tail.

Recovering quickly from the shock and amazement of what he had witnessed, Michael raced to Cassie's side. He took her hand. As he laced his fingers through hers, their gazes met. Energy and need swept through him like dual lightning bolts. He felt caught by the storm, driven by a force much stronger than the wind buffeting the tops of the trees.

Twice in as many hours they had escaped death. They'd survived the rapids and now a bear attack. The feeling of invincibility swelled in him, growing, expanding, until he was filled with power. He exalted in the sensation. He wanted to conquer the world. He wanted to...

His gaze traveled across Cassie's upturned face, her seductive mouth, the pert tilt of her nose, her eyes sparkling with excitement. He wanted to see those sweet, sexy eyes darkened with passion, reflecting the same kind of gut-wrenching need that heated and quickened his blood.

Lightning flashed again; thunder shook the ground. In the distance, the bear bellowed in fury.

"The cabin," he ordered. His breath came in shallow gasps. His heart labored. He would have Cassie. Soon. "While we can make it."

Never letting go of her hand, he led Cassie at a run back along the trail whence they had come. Sheeting rain turned to hail, pelting them with rock-hard stones, some the size of goose eggs. He shrugged off the bruising blows.

Cassie slipped on a slick combination of hail and mud, then recovered her balance as Michael pulled her relentlessly toward the cabin. She held one arm over her head to ward off the pounding stones. Wind whipped at her hair; thunder assaulted her senses. The unnatural maelstrom churned all around her, picking up fallen debris from the ground and tossing it recklessly in their path.

They burst into the clearing. As though determined to force them back into the woods, the wind screamed and swirled. The cabin seemed like an impossibly distant haven.

Cassie leaned into the storm. Deep in her heart she believed as long as she held Michael's hand she would be safe, her fears would remain at bay.

He covered the ground in powerful, sure strides. Once there, he tried the latch. When nothing happened he rammed his shoulder against the door once, and then again. On the third try, a powerful effort that shook the cabin, the barrier gave way. They staggered inside and slammed the door shut behind them, dropping the latch back in place.

Heavy log walls muted the fury of the storm outside. The wind whined a keening sound as it circled the cabin, rattling the chimney, attacking any crack it could find in the sturdy shelter. She could see little in the single room, only dim shapes of a table and chairs, a potbellied stove, something that looked as if it might be a bed against one wall.

Cassie shivered. Icy rainwater dripped down the back of her neck.

He pulled her into his arms. His voice hoarse, he groaned, "My God, Cassie..." There was a wildness about him, a primitive energy she hadn't seen before. His dark eyes flashed with the same undeniable potency as the storm they had just escaped. In a gesture that spoke eloquently of passion near the bursting point, he fisted a handful of her hair and tilted her head back. His mouth came down on hers with bruising urgency.

At the first thrust of his tongue, a matching primal urge uncoiled within her. She tasted his heat, savored it, and stole the oxygen from his lungs to feed the flames that flared within her. She shifted against him. His arousal pressed into her belly and she rejoiced.

"Cassie," he said thickly, placing one kiss after another on her face and along the sensitive column of her neck. "I want you."

The answer filled her throat, a feeling deep from within her heart. "I want you, too."

"I want this to be right for you."

"It will be." She measured the breadth of his shoulders with her hands, felt the power of the muscles that corded his neck.

"We should go slowly."

"No. Hurry. That's how much I want you." She trembled with the desire to touch him all over, to feel him fill her, satisfy her. She'd already waited too long. A lifetime, it seemed.

"I swear, Cassie, I'll stop if you tell me to." His voice strained with the effort to contain his emotion. "Somehow I'll stop."

"I'd never ask you to stop. Never."

Driven by an urgency more powerful than she'd ever experienced, she stripped him of his shirt and palmed the taut flesh across his chest. His rain-soaked skin was covered by gooseflesh that she warmed with her hands. She drew in his heady, masculine scent at the same time she felt his strong hands tug her T-shirt upward, past her midriff, skimming her breasts and then off over her head. At the sight of the lacy covering hiding her breasts, a predatory smile, hungry and demanding, lifted his lips. The low, rough sound he made sent a shiver of shameless excitement through her. In the next instant, he had expertly removed her bra. The wisp of nylon fabric dropped silently to the floor.

She almost sobbed at the pleasure of his rough hands cupping her breasts. His breathing raspy, he dipped his head to suckle first one nipple and then the other. His tongue warmed them like a flame touched to a candle; his teeth punished the tender flesh into aching beads of sensual delight.

Her fingers dug into his scalp to bring him closer, urging him to take her more fully. She arched up to him. His dark, damp hair weighted the back of her hands like heavy, sensuous threads.

"Michael..." she moaned. Her call mixed with the sound of the wind still swirling around the cabin.

"You taste so good."

His deft fingers worked the snap free on her jeans. The zipper slid down with a quick rasp and then his hands lowered her pants to her thighs. She clung to him. The wooden table felt cold and hard against the back of her legs as he lifted her from her feet. He settled her hips on the rustic planks.

While he worked to remove her boots and jeans, she touched him, learning the texture of the burnished skin across his back, its warmth, the movement of his muscles, glorious details she sought to memorize. He was ruggedly beautiful, a powerful male, every line of his body streamlined and meant for a woman to love.

His fingers roughly kneaded her inner thigh. She gasped. Desire rocketed from the point of contact to the apex of her womanhood.

She couldn't seem to catch her breath. Her heart battered against her rib cage, an echo of the hail pelting the roof to the cabin. "Please hurry," she urged.

In a swift, fluid motion, he lowered his jeans.

His naked body was magnificent. She felt the press of him between her legs, and then he was within her, filling her with stroke after vigorous stroke. She'd waited so long, had dreamed so long of this very moment.

As though she was in the middle of a whirlwind, she was caught up in the sensations. The slight roughness of his thighs rubbing against the tender flesh along the inside of hers. His hands cupping and lifting her hips, kneading and urging her on. The feel of his tongue dancing with hers. His musky, masculine scent an aphrodisiac to all of her senses. She felt herself spinning out of control.

Michael couldn't get enough of her. His need was a savage thing. Hooking his arms beneath her legs, he leaned her back onto the table.

Thoughts he hadn't dared allow himself flared into urgent need. Simple craving became urgent need.

He felt her tightened around him, rippling with passion on the verge of release. In that one brief moment before they flew over the brink together, he looked into her eyes. He saw the naked need in her. Her vulnerability. The shockingly tender feelings he experienced were at complete odds with the rough way he was taking her. But there was no going back; no stopping.

He called out her name in a prayer to ancient spirits, as fundamental as the earth and sky, and felt himself shatter with a force as powerful as those that created the universe.

Chapter Nine

The freak summer storm had abated, though the rain continued to drum steadily on the cabin roof and darkness was creeping in through the single, narrow window.

Cassie sat on the edge of the bed with a coarse wool blanket wrapped around her bare shoulders. She shivered as she watched Michael stuff kindling into the potbellied stove. He'd pulled his still-damp jeans back on, but he was still bare chested, his bronzed flesh the kind of skin a woman needed to caress. Cassie's fingers itched to do just that.

He moved with quiet masculine grace, the image of male perfection. She wished he'd hurry with the fire. She wanted to be held again as he'd held her all too briefly after their passionate lovemaking, only long enough to allow the sated languor that had seeped into her body to vanish and be replaced with desire once again. She felt an insatiable appetite to know Michael one more time, though she doubted once more would ever be enough.

He struck a match and the wood caught. The flames flickered, sending a sensuous play of light across his rugged features. Dark. Mysterious. Incredibly desirable.

He turned, his expression guarded. The look in his eyes bored through Cassie's blanket to heat every inch of her skin. "I'm sorry, Cassie." His voice was low and husky, unfairly sexy, and thick with emotion. "I don't know what got into me."

Sorry? The word flayed her like a whip. Her breath caught at the pain. Swallowing hard, she lifted her chin. "My Aunt Myrtle used to say a body didn't have enough time on this earth to waste on regrets. Frankly, I thought the whole experience was pretty darn exciting."

In two quick strides, he was across the room. He pulled her roughly to her feet. Startled, she clasped the blanket together at her neck. Her eyes widened.

"I didn't mean I was sorry we made love," he amended. "It's just that I've never lost control like that before."

Grinning impudently, she said, "Maybe the next time we could go a *little* bit slower." Maybe they could hang around together for thirty or forty years, making love until they got it just right. "But not too slow," she warned. "I wouldn't want to bore you."

His large, roughened hands formed tender parentheses around her face. "Cassie, it's entirely possible you could drive me crazy, but never in a million years would you ever, ever bore me."

She felt the renewed flutter of excitement low in her belly. "Should I take that as a compliment?"

He groaned. "Hell, yes." His mouth captured hers in a kiss as hot and needy as those they had shared only minutes ago. Cassie drank in his familiar flavor, a tangy elixir of love.

As though the power of the storm outside had been renewed, the cabin door burst open, slamming back against the wall with a crash.

Fear sliced through the scream that rose in Cassie's throat.

In the doorway, an apparition in a yellow rain slicker and matching hat held a shotgun pointed right at them.

"I don't abide no trespassers," the vision announced. Without lowering the shotgun, the woman stepped into the cabin, removed her drooping hat and shook the rain from it. Lank, gray hair hung to her shoulders and her narrow face was so wrinkled it looked like a road map of downtown Minneapolis. "What are you young folks doin' in my place?"

Michael positioned himself protectively between Cassie and the old woman. "A bear was chasing us, ma'am. We came inside because it was the only safe place around.''

"It wasn't just a bear, ma'am," Cassie tried to explain. "It was more like something terribly evil."

"Humph. Ol' Willie's evil, all right, but he ain't anything 'cept a mean ol' bear. Thought I heard him hollerin' and carryin' on. You musta been the burr what got under his skin this time." She dropped her hat on the plank table and studied the two of them through squinted eyes. "Found a canoe down by the lake. You the travelers?"

"Yes, ma'am," Cassie replied. "We're on our way to Way Quah."

The woman's scrutiny grew more intense, and Cassie felt a blush creep up her neck as the cabin's owner noticed the way her clothes were strewn higgledy-piggledy across the room.

"Looks to me like you got waylaid doing somethin' else."

"We were both soaked through from the storm," Michael explained. "I didn't want Cassie to catch a chill."

"I just bet." She cocked her head skeptically, then lowered the shotgun. "Reckon that's your business, not mine. Shut the door, young man, and I'll get you some root beer. Make it myself. Fifty cents a glass, it is. Paid in advance. Dinner's a buck and so's staying overnight. And 'lessen you two are married to each other, there ain't gonna to be no hanky-panky in my place. You got that?''

Cassie shot Michael a guilty look.

"We don't want to trouble you, ma'am," he said. "We'll just camp down by the lake."

"I wouldn't. That ol' Willie is a mean son of a gun. Takes him a while to cool off once he's riled." Working with weather-roughened hands and fingers gnarled with arthritis, she busied herself lighting an old kerosene lantern that hung above the table. When the wick caught, it gave off more smoke than light.

Holding the blanket around her as best she could, Cassie slipped across the room to Michael. Taking his hand, she whispered, "I think she probably needs the money. I'd be willing to spend the night if you don't mind." Her gaze shot with regret to the bed along the wall. The realization that they wouldn't be able to make love while they stayed in the cabin was a serious disappointment. A moment ago she'd been planning for an encore, a comfortable one where they could stretch out together.

He looped his arm around her waist in a possessive gesture that suggested he might be having similar thoughts. The physical recollection of his rigid male flesh filling her to the hilt brought a gasp to her lips that she swallowed back with a sigh.

"I don't even know why she's living out here all alone, Cassie. It doesn't make any sense. Chances are she's got a few screws loose."

"Only because she's lonely. Anybody would be a little odd living like this. I know Flossie, one of my regulars at the coffee shop, sometimes acts funny. I think it's because she goes days without talking to anybody. One night here won't hurt us, and maybe the old woman can tell us the way to the enchanted village."

With a doubtful shake of his head, he said, "Do I really have a choice?"

She grinned up at him, so filled with love she thought she might burst. "Nope. But thank you for asking."

A responding smile tugged at the corners of his lips, sending a flutter of excitement right to Cassie's midsection. Maybe this was a bad idea. Curled up together in the tent sounded like a much more fun way to spend the night. Assuming the bear didn't show up again.

That thought gave her pause. She'd been so sure there was something truly evil about the bear . . . and something very unnatural about the storm. Maybe even mystical. But now . . . She simply wasn't sure.

"I'll go get our gear," Michael said.

Distracted, she nodded. "I guess that's best."

"No need." The old woman shoved a couple of pieces of split pine into the stove then hung her slicker on a wall peg. She wore a heavy flannel shirt of faded plaid stuffed into canvas overalls. Her heavy boots were mud caked. "Already brung up your bedrolls. They're right outside the door. Figured you'd stay. Most travelers do, 'specially on rainy nights that ain't fit for man nor beast." She glanced around the cabin, pride obvious in her gray eyes. "Welcome. The name's Annie. Annie Kincaid. My friends, what few I got left of 'em, call me Grannie."

CASSIE CHOKED ON HER first sip of root beer. Coughing, she glanced across the table and caught Michael's amused expression. No telling what kind of "roots" Grannie had used to make this concoction. It would serve him right if she poured the whole mug of bitter brew over his head.

Instead she said, "This is wonderful, Grannie. I'm sure Michael will want a second cupful."

"It'd be another fifty cents. Can't be giving it away, you know. A woman has to look out fer herself first."

"Thanks, anyway," he sputtered. "I think one cup will be my limit for tonight. Don't want to overdo a good thing."

He gave Cassie a dirty look, which she shrugged off with a smug smile. The wool shirt she'd borrowed from Grannie while her own clothes were drying near the fire smelled slightly of mildew. It hung nearly to her knees, covering her bottom but leaving her legs bare. Curling her toes, she crossed one cold foot over the other.

"Have you lived here long, Grannie?" Cassie asked as the woman ladled a heap of beans on each of three chipped china plates.

"Reckon it's been sixty or more years, give or take a few." She sliced and added a large hunk of bread to the plates.

"You've been alone all that time?"

"'Sakes, no. Folks come by maybe once or twice a year."

"Are they people who are searching for Way Quah?"

The old woman eyed Cassie suspiciously. "Some is. Some ain't. You said that's where you're headed?"

"Yes. Michael is taking me there."

She slid the plates onto the table.

"I'm a licensed guide," he explained. He studied the meal she'd placed in front of him, suspecting the coagulated heap of beans wasn't likely to taste much better than the homemade root beer.

"Phooey. A guide's no use in finding Way Quah," the old woman complained.

"Then you know where it is?" Cassie asked. Her beautiful blue eyes sparkled with eagerness and the undeniable conviction of a true believer. Her enthusiasm brought a bright glow to her carefully sculpted cheeks and made Michael hungry for her all over again.

"Nope. Ain't never tried to go there and don't plan to, neither."

"But why not? It's supposed to be an enchanted, wonderful place. It must be nearby or you wouldn't have had so many people looking for it."

"Fools, I calls 'em. But maybe they ain't heard the same tales as me." She frowned, her forehead pleating like waves on the lake during a storm.

Michael didn't like the old woman's ominous tone. "You think it's dangerous?" How, he wondered, could a myth be dangerous?

"Reckon." She forked some beans into her mouth.

"What makes you think so?" he persisted.

"Evil. It's all around out there. And witches. Strange things happen for no reason." She washed her beans down with a big swig of root beer and grimaced. "Them what keeps on goin' like as not will get kilt, horrible like."

"Oh, you're just trying to scare us," Cassie said, dismissing the woman's concerns with an easy smile. "Way Quah holds the secret of happiness."

Grannie shook her fork at Cassie. "Now you listen to me, child. You two young'uns would be smart to take my advice. Go on back where you come from, you hear?"

Shaking her head, Cassie said, "We've come this far and we're not going to let bogeyman stories scare us off. Or bears or white-water rapids, or anything else. Are we, Michael?"

The need to please Cassie, to see the same passion she had for Way Quah in her eyes when she looked at him, twisted through Michael's gut.

Reaching across the table, he covered her small, delicate hand with his. She had more courage and determination in one finger than most people had in their whole body. Stubbornness, too. He admired her for all of her wonderful attributes, even envied her eternal optimism, but he was a rational man. At least, he had been until Cassie came along. And he hated the thought that in the long run she would be disappointed.

"Maybe we ought to listen to her, Cassie." Not that he believed Grannie's stories any more than the superstitious tales he had heard as a child.

Her chin quivered and disappointment filled her eyes. "What I start, I like to finish. There are folks who are counting on me. And you promised...."

He squeezed her hand. "Yeah, I did." Fool that he was.

THE LAST GLOW OF FLAMES in the potbellied stove flickered out. Wide-eyed, Cassie lay in her bedroll on the hard-packed dirt floor of the cabin and listened to Grannie snoring like a lumberjack going through the forest with a chain saw. Next to Cassie, Michael stirred restlessly.

"You asleep?" she whispered.

"With that racket going on? Not a chance."

Giggling softly, she reached out for him. Their hands met and clasped in the darkness, his thumb gently caressing her knuckles. "Poor thing must have an adenoid problem."

"Terrific. I really feel sorry for her. But frankly, my problem's a whole hell of a lot more painful."

"What's wrong?" Cassie had no idea Michael had been hurt, maybe in his flight from the bear, she thought.

"I can't seem to turn off my libido. I ache for you, Cassie," he said in his raspy, sexy way. "I have since we made love this afternoon. House rules or not, I can't seem to stop wanting you."

His admission spiraled through her with dizzying pleasure. "I want you, too," she admitted, her voice little more than a hoarse groan of frustration. She brought his hand to her face and rubbed her cheek along the strong contours of his knuckles, wanting to purr like a cat who loved to be stroked. She kissed him, tasting the tangy flavor of his salty skin.

He sucked in a breath. "Cassie..." His fingers played through her hair, threading lightly through the strands, then kneading her scalp. Clasping his wrist, she leaned into his touch. She squirmed within the narrow confines of her bedroll.

"Michael, I wish we could—"

"Yeah, I know." He rolled over in his bedroll to lie half on top of her, his weight pressing her down into the softness of her sleeping bag. His lips were hot against the shell of her ear. "If it weren't for Grannie, you know what I'd do to you?"

In a hoarse whisper he told her how and where he would kiss her. Shockingly private places. Places that burned at the very thought of being touched so intimately. Cassie's pulse surged, ticking wildly at the sensitive spot on the column of her neck and throbbing much lower in her body. A soft moan rose in her throat.

"You're driving me crazy," she protested.

"You've been doing that to me since you first showed up at my workshop." His teeth captured the tender flesh of her earlobe, giving her a sharp nip before kissing away the pain. "And if Grannie weren't here, I'd show you what else we could do besides kiss."

He told her in a grainy voice how he would ultimately take her, in positions she'd only imagined until now. With his words he drew vivid images, making her think about his rigid male flesh and how it would feel when they made love again. Her insides went all soft and wanting; her breathing accelerated. She desperately wanted to escape the confines of her bedroll and give substance to her wildly racing imagination.

He continued his verbal assault on her senses. No man had ever spoken to her in that way, made love to her with words so descriptive she could feel his hands on her, his tongue skimming her most private sanctuaries, his sure, strong thrusts that had the power to send her into ecstasy. She had no idea where he had learned such things. She simply wanted him to do everything he described . . . to her.

The realization that there was someone else in the room compounded the forbidden thrill of excitement. Fear of discovery, of being overheard, pumped added adrenaline through her veins. He played her with his erotic suggestions like a puppet on a string, making her body jump to his slightest command.

Battered sensually by his talented onslaught, she surrendered to the moment. Before she could tell Michael to stop, his hot, demanding mouth kissed hers and she trembled from the impact.

Sighing, Cassie thought maybe tomorrow she'd feel embarrassed by what they'd done in someone else's home, by the words Michael had spoken. But not now. She was simply feeling too content to worry about anything else.

Curling up on her side, she reached for Michael's hand and linked her fingers through his.

THE NEXT MORNING, with the mist still hugging the ground and lacing itself through the treetops, Cassie knelt next to the canoe. Her spirits plummeted and grief constricted her chest.

"How could I have forgotten about poor Ernie?" She held up a few straggly strips of bandages that looked as if they'd been dragged through the mud. The blue portage packs from the canoe had been batted around the sandy beach as if they were nothing more than toys. Her cans of exposed film dotted the ground, still safely sealed, thank goodness. Her camera and the heavy first-aid kit remained intact.

Michael's hand closed gently over her shoulder. "If you hadn't saved the mink from that rock slide, he wouldn't have lived this long. Some other predator would have gotten him. Minks don't usually have a very long life span."

"I know," she said with a sigh. "I just wish I hadn't left him here alone. He must have been so scared." She swallowed hard against the tears that threatened.

"There isn't any blood," Michael pointed out, obviously trying to restore her spirits. "Knowing Ernie, he probably chewed off his bandages and went exploring on his own."

Clucking a sympathetic sound, Grannie said, "A body cain't do much when ol' Willie gets on a rampage. 'Lessen I miss my guess, that's the villain what made this mess. You two young folks were lucky to get away with your hides in one piece."

Cassie tended to agree. Still, it was hard to admit her carelessness had cost poor little Ernie his life. She hoped Michael was right about the mink making his escape.

Standing, she rubbed at the small of her back and rotated her aching shoulders. Sleeping on a hard-packed dirt floor hadn't been all that comfortable.

She looked across the lake. The mist hovered all the way down to the water. Not a breath of wind moved through the air, no breeze disturbed the still, gray, seamless expanse of water and sky. The opposite shore lay hidden from view, a secret, mystical place shrouded by the fog. Like vapor rising off the surface of the quiet lake, images came to her, indistinct, but she sensed in her heart they were real. She caught the scent of cooking fires and heard the bantering of families laughing together as they greeted the new day, the bark of a dog.

A smile of accomplishment formed deep inside her, rose insistently, and she *knew*. She'd reach her goal. Way Quah lay only minutes away.

CLOUDS THE COLOR of pewter misted the quiet lake as Michael dipped his paddle into the water and pulled toward the opposite shore. They'd left Grannie on the beach muttering dire warnings. He could sense Cassie's building excitement as they drew closer to their destination. From her spot in the bow, she leaned forward, peering through the fog. She fussed anxiously with her camera then checked their slow progress. Michael regretted the disappointment she faced.

There was no Way Quah. Ancient storytellers intent on entertaining their listeners, plus dream-induced fantasies, were the source of the myth. Even the warnings of evil witches Grannie had spouted were no more than figments of someone's imagination.

He picked a landing place midway between two giant white pines. There was no sign of life along the shore, no well-worn path; no distant sounds drifted through the woods. Eerie stillness pressed down on the wilderness. They were alone.

Once on shore, he stood with Cassie, his arm around her waist. She felt soft and womanly, and he wanted to hold her again, all day and all night, and desperately wanted to protect her from disappointment. "I'm sorry," he said. "This is the end of the line."

She looked up at him with bright, eager eyes and she smiled. "I know. Isn't it wonderful? Right through those trees we'll find the village."

"No, Cassie. There's nothing here. Only the two of us and a forestful of trees."

She palmed his face, her hand delicate and warm on his cheek. "You're wrong. I can hear them laughing."

Michael figured she must be listening to a frequency that was well beyond his range of hearing. He only heard the lap of water against the shore. The cold, misty weather had even vanquished the insistent hum of mosquitoes.

Slowly, he shook his head.

"Michael, I trusted you when I was dangling at the end of a rope a hundred feet off the ground. I didn't doubt for a minute when we were in those rapids that you'd get us through them in one piece...."

"I'd lost my paddle, remember?"

"And I knew, evil or not, we'd somehow get away from that crazed bear." She lowered her voice to a husky, intimate whisper, her emotions so intense he could feel them burrowing under his skin. "I trusted you even more so yesterday when we made love," she pointed out. "Fair is fair. Now it's time for you to believe in me."

He wanted to. For the first time in many years, Michael wanted to believe in Way Quah. Not for himself. For Cassie. He couldn't bear the thought of seeing her lovely, eager eyes filled with disillusion, her sweet, mobile mouth shaped by disappointment. He wouldn't be able to stand the pain.

He tipped his hat to the back of his head. Clasping her shoulders, he placed a soft, hungry kiss on her lips. "You win, Cassie. You always do. Go ahead. Show me. Lead me to the village."

She beamed him a smile so radiant the clouds seemed to lift from the treetops. Sunlight sliced through the branches, dappling the ground with shadows, and birds began to sing.

Taking his hand and laughing, she pulled him into the woods. "Come on then, slowpoke. Last one to the village has to eat worms."

Chuckling, Michael realized Cassie had an uncanny ability to make him feel young and unstoppable, as though he could climb the highest mountain or run the longest race without ever getting winded. He suspected she had the same effect on others, like the friends she spoke about at the coffee shop. He could only assume she'd been born with that special gift. He envied her.

He figured he had far less to give to Cassie than he gave to him. And that, he knew, was the ultimate in unfairness.

They made their own path through the trees. When the pines and damp undergrowth grew too thick for passage, Cassie simply found an easier route. When the ground became too boggy, she sought and guided them to solid footing with unerring accuracy. She ran as lightly as a dancer, skimming effortlessly past birches with leaves just beginning to show their autumn color. Her feet hardly seemed to touch the ground. Her absolute conviction that Way Quah lay just around the next tree or bush gave her buoyancy. Her belief would not be denied.

Yet Michael faltered once again at the impossibility of her goal. Tripping over a root, he lost his grip on Cassie's hand. In an instant so quick it was less than a heartbeat, he knew there was no Way Quah without her. Then the mist closed oppressive and thick around him.

When Cassie felt Michael's hand slip away, she whirled. He was gone. Vanished somewhere into the gray mist. Panic assailed her and a vast feeling of loneliness pressed painfully in on her breastbone. She had never felt so alone.

"Michael!" she cried. "Come back. Please."

He heard her call. Relief and renewed determination to grant Cassie's dream surged through him as he shoved his way through a tight maze of pines toward the sound of her voice. Needled tree branches whipped at his face.

Shouldering his way, he broke out into a clearing where Cassie stood.

She greeted him with a heart-stopping smile and an outstretched hand. "Oh, Michael, I thought I'd lost you."

"I'm here, Cassie." Emotion tightened the muscles in his throat.

As their fingers linked, they turned together and rushed through a stand of trees, out of the forest into a fragrant meadow awash with sunlight.

The feeling of dèjá vu slammed into Michael with the force of a sledgehammer. He'd been here before. His adolescent vision quest had brought him to exactly this same spot. It wasn't possible. Yet that's what his eyes, and his heart, told him.

Chapter Ten

The laughter of playing children filled the air, a joyous sound that seemed to glisten in the same way sunlight sparkles across a lake. A dozen wigwams placed in neat rows formed a rectangle that bordered the woods, and from each one smoke drifted lazily upward from cooking fires. The scent of roasting meat floated on the currents.

Cassie linked her arm through Michael's, so happy she thought she might explode.

From the center of the village a young woman walked toward them. She carried a toddler on her hip and a welcoming smile lit her face. Her hair was as jet black as Michael's, hanging past her shoulders in a silken fall like a raven's wing. Distinctively high cheekbones, innocent doe eyes and a slender nose gave her an exotic appearance.

Wearing a dress made of soft deerskin, the young mother moved with easy grace in spite of her advanced pregnancy. An exquisite medallion made of finely woven reeds dangled around her neck.

"Welcome to our village," she said in a voice as tranquil as a bubbling creek tumbling gently through a mountain glade. "My name is Running Deer, and this is my son, Laughing Mink."

"I'm just real happy to meet you. We both are." Barely able to contain herself, Cassie gestured to include Michael in her acknowledgement. "We've come such a long way and, well... This is Way Quah, isn't it?"

"If that is what you would like it to be." Cassie thought the young woman's smile had the same enigmatic quality as the woman in the *Mona Lisa*.

"Sure I do. I mean, I've been wanting to come here since I was just a little kid. My Aunt Myrtle said if I kept thinking about it and kept trying hard enough, someday I'd make it. And, well..." She took a deep breath. Her face muscles ached, she was grinning so hard. "Here I am."

"I am glad you and your friend could make the journey. For many, the trip is too difficult."

"Oh, I couldn't have made it without Michael to help me." She squeezed his arm and looked up at him with adoring eyes. In spite of his amazed expression, he looked extra handsome with his hat sitting to the back of his head at a cocky angle. Lord, how she wanted this man. Her body still tingled at the very thought of how they had made such urgent, reckless love, and the promise of more to come.

"Yes, he would know the way."

At the sound of her softly spoken words, Cassie returned her attention to Running Deer. The child in her arms stared at her with dark, soulful eyes, then squirmed to get free. His mother lowered him to the ground. He ran with a limp as he dashed out of sight.

His mother watched his progress, a frown marring her otherwise flawless features. "We had thought my son's leg was broken but found it was only a bad sprain. He will be well soon. And, I suspect, even more difficult to handle," she admitted with an affectionate smile. "Laughing Mink is well named. He is often more mischievous than most children his age."

Cassie caught Michael's incredulous expression. She knew what he was thinking and she felt an unsettled feeling in her stomach. But no, that wasn't possible. It was only coincidence that the little boy's eyes resembled those of both Ernies—the lost mink and her friend from the coffee shop—and the child had an injured leg. It couldn't be anything more than odd happenstance.

"If you will please come with me I will show you where you may stay while you are visiting us," Running Deer invited. "The chief of our village, Gray Wolf, and my husband, Night Hawk, are away on a hunting trip, or I am sure they would be here to offer you the hospitality of the village. Perhaps they will return before you must leave.''

''I hope so, Running Deer. We're excited about meeting everybody.''

As they followed her past a wigwam where a woman sat cross-legged stringing beads, Cassie nudged Michael in the ribs. ''Isn't this perfect? I knew Way Quah would be like this. It even smells wonderful. Spices and wood smoke and meat sizzling over a fire. And look how happy everyone is.''

''Doesn't it seem just a little too perfect, Cassie?'' he warned grimly. ''So idyllic that it can't be real?''

''Oh, stop being such an ol' grump, Michael Longlake. The village is beautiful and we're here and nothing else matters.'' Cassie kept her arm firmly hooked through his. If she had her way, they'd spend the rest of their lives together in a place like Way Quah. Or at least a place where they could be with each other.

With every step she took, she absorbed the energy of the village, noting how families worked and played contentedly together. Young children roamed freely under the watchful eye of any nearby adult. When a toddler tripped over his own feet a preadolescent girl scooped the crying, bare-bottomed youngster into her arms and dusted off his dirty knees. Adding to the general confusion in the village, an assortment of dogs played with the children, yapping at their heels.

The love in the village seemed a palpable thing, like the scent of wildflowers in the air or the sound of wood doves calling quietly from the trees. It made Cassie ache to have her own family, to have a husband she loved and a child nestling in her lap...a child much like these who looked at her shyly, their dark eyes questioning and curious. A child, she realized with a swift intake of air, with Michael's onyx eyes, raven hair and a smile the tiny replica of his.

Instinctively, her free hand covered her belly. Perhaps at this very moment Michael's baby grew within her, taking nourishment from her body that would make him as strong and tall as his father. She could imagine nothing that would bring her more joy.

She glanced at Michael, at his rugged features and the stern set of his jaw. With a sinking feeling she realized he might not share her happiness at the thought of starting a new family with her. After all, she'd kind of blasted her way into his life and dragged him on an adventure.

As doubts assailed her, Cassie's footsteps faltered. Her confidence slipped, and as it did the village wavered before her eyes like a mirage on a summer day. Images pulsated in and out of focus.

"Are you all right?" Michael asked.

She clung to his arm more tightly. "Yes, I'm fine," she lied. In her heart of hearts, she was suddenly more scared than she had ever been in her life. The experience was more frightening than dangling from a rope a hundred feet in the air, more terrifying than being chased by a crazed bear. She plumbed her depths for a new dose of confidence. Somehow she had to go on believing everything would be fine, that in Way Quah she would find the secret to happiness.

Running Deer glanced at them over her shoulder. "Before I show you where you will be staying, would you care for some refreshments?"

"Well, sure, if it's not any trouble," Cassie agreed. She wasn't exactly hungry, but she did have questions and hoped the distraction of conversation would give her a few minutes to steady herself.

The young woman veered to the right, to a wigwam that seemed slightly larger than the rest. In front of the structure sat an older, gray-haired woman sewing what looked to be a pair of moccasins, her gnarled fingers threading a needle through the soft fabric. She looked up as they approached. Her face was a map of age-worn wrinkles.

"This is my mother, Dawn's Light," Running Deer said as she introduced them.

"Pleased to meet you," Cassie said. She smiled a bit as she tried to remember who the woman reminded her of. Perhaps Eldyne Bowen at the coffee shop, but she couldn't quite be sure.

"*Bi-jou,*" Michael said, acknowledging the woman's greeting.

"Ah, you still remember the language of your people," the old woman said.

"A little," he conceded.

Running Deer gestured for them to be seated in front of the wigwam, then vanished out of sight.

Sitting cross-legged, Cassie settled herself with her back against the wigwam. Michael took a place opposite her, across an outdoor fire pit, and pulled his pipe from his jacket pocket. She watched as he filled the bowl with tobacco, tamped it down and struck a match. He looked very much at home in an Indian village. In some other lifetime he would have been a chief, she imagined. A powerful, well-respected leader.

Dawn's Light bit off a piece of thread, spit it out and studied her guests. "So you decided to come, in spite of those who told you it was dangerous."

"Yes, ma'am." Cassie adjusted her position to make herself more comfortable. "I've always wanted to visit Way Quah."

The woman snorted an unfriendly sound. "Some folks don't know when to stop asking for trouble."

Cassie wanted to ask what the woman meant, but Running Deer returned with a drink for each of them that smelled a bit like rose-hip tea. She took a sip. The sweet, warm liquid slid soothingly down her throat.

"Are you folks the Dream Catchers Michael told me about?" Cassie asked her hostess.

"Would that please you?" Running Deer replied noncommittally.

"Well, it's not so much that, but if you are, then my friends at the coffee shop where I work will be really excited to know I found you."

"I imagine they would be pleased simply to know you have traveled so far."

"Sure, that's true. But, see, you're supposed to be able to find the secret of happiness at Way Quah. At least, that's what I told them. And I imagine you know all about that." All of her favorite customers needed a helping hand one way or another to find happiness. She really wanted to find a sure cure to fix their problems. It was, after all, the reason she'd come so far.

"I am sure you and your friends already hold the secret you seek in your hearts. All you need do is recognize it."

Cassie glanced across the fire pit, catching Michael's eye. With a start, she realized *he* was her secret to happiness. What she had experienced in her life until now she could call contentment. Satisfying in many ways but only marking time. There was a whole higher threshold of experience, of feelings, she hadn't perceived until he had come into her life.

She blew out a sigh. Convincing Michael they belonged together was probably the most challenging task she'd ever undertaken. Lord help her, it was the only one that mattered.

One of the village dogs, an old mongrel that looked to be part wolf, belly crawled up next to Michael and rested his head on Michael's thigh. He whined softly.

To Cassie's surprise, Michael tensed momentarily before petting the animal.

The dog's tail swept a contented path across the dirt, and Cassie wondered what had brought the sudden scowl to Michael's face.

SEVERAL HOURS LATER, Running Deer led them to a wigwam that was much like the others in the village. Except for an open doorway, wide strips of birchbark circled the conical hut, each strip bound with cedar and sewed with basswood bark. Michael had lived parts of his childhood in such a structure, often a temporary home and easily moved with the changing seasons. The sight brought back memories of the days he had spent gathering wild rice with his family. Happy times compared to those dreary months he lived away from his home at Indian school. Little wonder when he'd been hallucinating as a teenager that he'd conjured up the memory of a village like this.

For Cassie's sake, he forced himself to believe this version of Way Quah was real. It wasn't easy. Yet how could he rationally explain they were both hallucinating, both experiencing the same dream?

"I believe you will find all you need here," Running Deer said. She held back a buckskin drape that covered the doorway. "If you wish anything more, I will be near."

"Thanks so much, Running Deer. We're just real glad to be here," Cassie repeated. "Before we go inside, would you mind standing right there while I take your picture?"

"If that is your wish."

Michael watched as Cassie adjusted her camera. "Oh, shoot," she muttered. "Isn't that always the way? I've already used up the last picture on this roll. I must have accidentally snapped one when we were in the canoe." She rolled the end of the film through the camera and flipped open the back, saying, "Can you wait just one minute?"

"Of course." Running Deer stood patiently beside the wigwam, her hand resting at the small of her back, her expression serene. "Here there is all the time you need."

Cassie put the used roll in her pocket and inserted a fresh one in her camera. Her hands trembled a little, from excitement, Michael guessed.

"All my friends back home are going to be so anxious to see you and Way Quah. They've all been hearing me talk about this place till they're sick of me running off at the mouth, I'm sure. Arletta says I get stuck on something like a needle in an old long-play record and I just won't give up." She raised the camera to her eye. "Okay. Say parsnips."

Running Deer's composure slipped and she smiled broadly, her dark eyes glistening with fun.

"What ever happened to cheese?" Michael asked, amused but equally troubled by the feeling he'd met Running Deer before. There was something very familiar about her smile, something that tugged at the back of his mind like a dream that wouldn't quite let go.

Cassie insisted he stand next to Running Deer while she took another picture. He squinted into the sun, forcing a smile he didn't quite believe, and wondered if he reached out to touch Running Deer if he would find substance, or only the wispy remnants of a dream.

When the photo session was complete, the young woman left, and he and Cassie entered the wigwam.

An open fire pit in the center of the large room caught the light from the wide smoke hole at the peak of the ceiling. Dust motes danced in the column of sunlight. As a child, Michael had been taught that light cast into the wigwam by the Great Spirit brought good health. When his mother died of influenza he'd discovered sometimes that wasn't enough, just as he had later discovered his skills and modern medicine weren't always adequate to save those he loved.

At one side of the room a bed rested a foot above the ground on sturdy poles and was covered with deer pelts for warmth. The mattress, he knew, would be a soft bed of balsa branches.

All was as it should be, Michael realized, yet the details were too specific, so accurate he felt like he was in a museum. Or experiencing a dream. How could he explain it to Cassie without destroying her spirit?

Pulling her back from the explorations of the wigwam, Michael said, "Sweetheart, did you notice Running Deer didn't actually say this was Way Quah?"

"Well, of course she did. What else could this place be way out here in the middle of the wilderness right where the map said it was?"

"We don't even know quite where we are. Maybe this is only an ordinary Chippewa village, and they've gathered here waiting for the time to harvest the wild rice."

"Don't be silly, Michael. We've traveled dozens of miles to get here, and there's nothing ordinary about this place. Besides, I've read lots of books on Native American history and there's no doubt in my mind that this is Way Quah. I'm sure it is."

"You're wrong," he stated bluntly.

Wincing at his sharp tone, she turned her head away. "After all we've been through together, how can you say—"

"I've been here before, Cassie."

Her incredulous gaze snapped back to meet his. "Here? At Way Quah? Why didn't you tell me?"

Taking her hand, he led her to the bed and they sat down beside each other. The layered deer pelts gave way beneath their weight. "I was fourteen years old. My mother had died several years before that and I was pretty messed up, driving my father and grandfather crazy and flunking school. Not to mention the fights every day after classes." He'd been on a razor edge when his grandfather's stories of his ancestry had brought him up short. "I went on a vision quest trying to find out who I was."

Her forehead furrowed. "I'm not sure I know what a vision quest is."

"It means I went out into the boundary waters alone. I had my canoe and a little beef jerky to eat. Nothing more. After a few days of hunger gnawing in my belly and a hundred hours of saying prayers beneath a tree, I was ready to believe anything.''

"And did you find what you were looking for?" she asked quietly.

"At the time, I thought I had found my way. I made an accommodation between my people's past and what I saw in the present. I believed I could bring the two parts of my life together. I had hoped to find happiness." He hesitated, painful memories twisting through his gut. "What I had discovered was nothing more than an illusion. That's all Way Quah is, Cassie. An illusion. There are no secrets to happiness."

With surprising strength, she squeezed his hands. "We're here, aren't we? I can feel the calluses on your hands. I can smell the charcoal in the fireplace and still hear the children playing outside the wigwam. And I can certainly feel what's in my heart. Isn't that all that matters?" Her eyes pleaded with him to understand, to believe.

Michael couldn't. Conflicting emotions pulled at him across time. He wanted Cassie. No way could he deny that fact. But he had a past he couldn't forget.

"Please, Michael, make love to me," she said in a low, scratchy voice. "Now. Here in the enchanted village I've dreamed about all of my life. Then both of us will know it's real."

"There are things about me you don't know," he cautioned. "You may not want—"

"It doesn't matter." Her breath hitched and he knew he owed her more than the quick coupling they had shared together. She deserved so much. He wished he were the man capable of fulfilling all of her dreams.

Cassie waited breathlessly for Michael's decision. His onyx gaze was so intense his eyes made her think of dark, hot coals. "You promised you'd kiss me. All over," she reminded him past the tightening in her throat. "I think a man ought to keep a promise like that, don't you?"

"When you look at me the way you are now, it's hard not to."

"My Aunt Myrtle used to say hesitatin' can stop a body from enjoying what life offers. That seems like worthwhile advice." Maybe not always, but today Cassie would agree. She crossed her arms and tugged her shirttail from her jeans, lifting the fabric over her head.

Michael's breathing deepened as he stared at the pale half moons of her breasts rising from her black, lacy bra. "Foolish, brave woman." With the back of one finger he slowly traced the scalloped edge of the nylon. Goose bumps rose on her flesh.

"I've always been the kind to go after what I wanted," she whispered. "No sense to keep your ambitions a secret."

The corners of his lips twitched. "And your ambition is for us to make love?"

"Yes." That was only the beginning, of course, but Cassie would let him get used to her dreams one step at a time. In her heart she had their whole lifetime planned together.

"Maybe you ought to set your sights higher."

She pointedly let her gaze drop from his eyes to his lap, to the obvious bulge pulling his jeans tautly across his thighs. "For now, I think my aim is pretty darn good right where it is."

Her retort galvanized Michael into action. He didn't have time to deal with illusions, only the ache in his loins. With a swift twisting motion, he pressed her down onto the bed of fur pelts and pinned her hands above her head. "You're a tempting she-devil, Cassie Seeger."

She grinned up at him. "I was afraid you wouldn't notice."

"Oh, I noticed," he growled.

Then he began kissing her, just as he had promised he would. Hot, tantalizing kisses. All over.

He began his assault on her mouth as he captured her lips, molding and shaping them to his design. Heat enveloped the tender inner flesh where he probed with his tongue. Swirling fire plundered her senses and she forgot how to breathe. Instantly out of control, she felt helpless to adequately respond. Her fingers combed through his hair of their own accord and kneaded the rippling muscles across his back. But the fire, the fire he created, followed the unrelenting path of his lips.

The barrier of clothing vanished. Flesh ignited at every sensitive spot—the indentation beneath her ear, the dip at the base of her throat, along the inside of her arms. She arched up to him time and again, seeking his fiery brand on every part of her body. He tortured her. Slowly. Incessantly. Denying her the ultimate heat of the rigid male flesh, the only thing that would ever be able to cool the inferno.

"Michael," she whispered hotly.

"I know. Tell me how it feels."

"Hot. Like I have . . . a fever." Even that description seemed inadequate to portray the intensity of what she was experiencing. Urgent need spiraled through her. Blood pounded through her veins and pooled at the throbbing point between her thighs. "Please, Michael . . ."

"I promised to go slowly this time."

"Yes . . . no. I can't . . ." She writhed beneath his onslaught.

As he kissed her in one intimate place after another, his dark hair grazed erotically against her flesh, sensitizing every nerve ending like the finest-grade sandpaper. How could she explain to Michael he had to hurry now or she'd burst into a thousand incandescent pieces? She sobbed his name again, dragging air painfully into her lungs.

Unwilling to be denied a moment longer, she wrapped her legs around his waist, pulling him toward her.

"Cassie..."

She exploded at the husky call of her name. A thousand flaming rockets rose into the sky and burst heavenward as she felt him fill her.

Chapter Eleven

Morning sounds filtered into the wigwam. Warblers called and squirrels carried on a heated argument in a nearby tree. A child cried and was hushed by its mother.

Cassie snuggled more tightly into Michael's embrace, cherishing the warmth of his naked flesh and his masculine strength. She rested her head on his shoulder, her arm draped across his broad chest. She'd never before understood references to the smell of sex. Now she did. The musky scent was all around them, in the air and clinging to their bodies. Even the pelts that covered them had absorbed the essence like an erotic perfume. She imagined she would always be able to remember the special fragrance she and Michael had created together.

She flicked the tip of her tongue across his flat nipple.

"Cassie," he groaned at her touch.

She loved the low, sexy way he said her name first thing in the morning.

He stirred and rubbed his hand along the small of her bare back. "I thought you'd be happy now that you've achieved your ambition. Several times over."

"Hmm. Temporarily." She'd lost count of the number of times they'd made love during the night. A delicious tenderness between her thighs attested to the fact there had been many.

"Frankly..." He adjusted his position to stretch his long, muscular legs. "I'm not sure I'll be able to walk anytime soon. I hope you have some other goal in life to distract you while I recover."

She smiled. Based on her limited knowledge, she figured Michael recovered at a Herculean rate. "I want to see and photograph everything here in Way Quah. That ought to keep me busy for a while." Not that she'd ever lose interest in other, more intimate pursuits.

"And then what, Cassie?" His raspy morning voice lowered another notch. "After we leave...after we wake up from this dream, or illusion, or whatever it is...and you go back to your coffee shop, what do you want to do?"

She swallowed hard. That wasn't exactly what she'd hoped to hear. It sounded too much like he was ready to get rid of her. How, after the way they'd spent the night together, could he *not* believe in Way Quah?

But her pride demanded she not ask him that.

"Arletta has talked about retiring some day. I've kind of hoped she might let me buy her out. On time, of course, from my wages. That way, eventually I'd have something to show for all my work." Granted, she'd give it all up in a minute if Michael asked her to help him make birchbark canoes, or better yet, asked her to help him spruce up that old Lakeside Lodge. She wouldn't mind all the hard work involved, particularly if Michael were there with her. Maybe that didn't make her sound like a woman of the nineties, to chuck her own dreams for a man, but that's exactly how she felt.

"You really enjoy waitressing that much?"

"I like the people." Each of the regulars, in their own way, needed her. She wished Michael could need her, too.

"No more treks scheduled in search of Cíbola, or some other exotic place?"

"I don't think so," she said softly. Any other adventure would pale in comparison to the reality of being with Michael. "Unless you want to come along?"

A low, rumbling laugh vibrated in his chest. "Not a chance."

His refusal hurt. More than she cared to admit, she realized. Suddenly she had to fight tears that burned at the back of her eyes. "We'd have a blast," she suggested, her voice catching in spite of herself.

Before he could reply, a scratching sound at the wigwam doorway preceded Running Deer's voice. "Whenever you wish breakfast, it is ready."

"We'll be there in a few minutes," Michael called.

Embarrassed heat swept up Cassie's neck. "I guess she knows what we've been doing."

"I imagine." Unconcerned, he unwrapped his long, lean body from the embrace they'd enjoyed. "Time to rise and shine, sweetheart."

From the corner of her eye, she watched as Michael got dressed and she did the same. With all her heart she tried to remember each rugged angle and plane of his body so she would never forget. Memories might be all she had left after her journey to Way Quah was complete.

LATER THAT MORNING Cassie sat with Running Deer, watching her weave a large mat from long reeds like those that grew in weedy spots around the edge of the lake. Her skilled hands moved quickly, and she worked without any apparent thought.

"Your man will return soon," Running Deer said in her soothing voice.

A twinge of guilt shifted Cassie's lips. "I wasn't thinking about Michael."

The woman's enigmatic smile suggested she thought otherwise.

"Well, maybe a little," Cassie conceded, grinning broadly. He'd only left a few minutes ago with a young Indian boy to set snares. She already missed him. "I've never known anyone quite like Michael."

"He is a good man, but he carries much pain in his heart."

"I know. I think it has something to do with how his wife died." Cassie stretched out her legs, crossed her ankles and braced herself on her hands, lifting her face to the sun. The sky was a glorious shade of blue and the air was as warm as a spring day.

"He has not told you the story?"

"No. I've been afraid to ask too many details for fear I'd push his misery button again. He gets real upset whenever I mention something about his family." And she didn't like bringing pain down on anyone.

"His memories are a deep festering wound that needs to be cleansed. You have the power to do that."

"You think so?" She'd be happy to spend a lifetime at the task if she thought she could help. "There's a guy who comes to the coffee shop—his name is Jack—who gets the same shadowed look in his eyes as Michael does sometimes. I don't know that I've been able to do much good for him.''

''But between you and this other man there is no love. With you and Michael it is different.''

''On my side of the fence that's true.'' Cassie wasn't at all sure about Michael's feelings. They might have *made* love half the night, but he hadn't said anything about being *in* love.

''You must find a way for Michael to tell you of his wounds so that they may heal.''

''Think so? I'm not sure he likes it when I stick my nose in his business. Maybe I ought to leave it alone.'' Things were going pretty well here at Way Quah. She hated to rock the boat.

Running Deer's hands stilled on her work. She sucked in a quick breath, and closed her eyes.

''Is there something wrong?'' Cassie asked, leaning toward her new friend in concern.

Slowly, Running Deer exhaled. ''My time approaches.''

''You mean you're going to have your baby?'' Cassie swallowed hard. ''Now? Should I go get help?''

''Not yet.'' The other woman fingered the medallion that rested above the swell of her pregnancy. Made of buckskin, the decoration was about six inches in diameter. Feathers and beads dangled from the sides and bottom of the circle; the center looked like a delicate spiderweb. "For the moment, the child only reminds me that his time will come soon."

"Well, when it happens, Michael's a paramedic. He could help you, I'm sure. He's real gentle with his hands."

"I will remember that. If the need arises." Running Deer returned to her work, her fingers deftly weaving the fibers together once again. Only a tightness around her lips revealed she was still experiencing discomfort.

"That's an interesting necklace you're wearing," Cassie observed, hoping to distract Running Deer from her pain.

"I wear this charm above where my child's heart beats so that he only has good dreams. See how the fine buckskin threads are a web to trap the evil spirits that visit in the night? Here, through this spirit hole in the center, only good dreams can flow." With her fingertip, she traced the small circle in the middle. "I would have my child happy."

A frown tightened Cassie's forehead. "Is that thing called a Dream Catcher?" It didn't look to her like a guardian for an enchanted village, but it certainly seemed to be the object's purpose. Maybe Michael had gotten the legend wrong.

"Some have called it so. If you wish, I will teach you to make one. It is not difficult."

"Well, maybe. But I don't know how long Michael will let us stay. He talked this morning like he was anxious to get back to work."

"Then there is much I must show you before you leave." Awkwardly, Running Deer levered herself to her feet.

Camera in hand, Cassie joined her for a guided tour of the village.

BY AFTERNOON, MICHAEL and the young Indian boy had returned to the village with a whole mess of partridges they had bagged. Cassie helped clean the birds and watched as Running Deer packed them in clay, then buried them in the hot ashes of the fire pit to cook.

For a time, Michael played a game that resembled lacrosse with some of the youngsters, then came to the edge of the field where Cassie had been watching. He'd stripped off his shirt at the beginning of the game, and his face and muscular torso were sheened with perspiration. He was breathing hard but there was a smile on his face.

"This is like coming home to the village of my youth," he said. "These boys are like those I played with as a kid. I know them all. Even their names."

"I told you Way Quah would be a wonderful place."

"It's still a dream, Cassie. But in this one I seem to be getting old. Can't quite keep up with those guys anymore." He slipped his arm possessively around her waist. He could understand a vision taking him back to happier times, to the village he remembered as a child, but the fact that he and Cassie were sharing the same illusion defied logic. "The kids are wearing me out."

"I don't think you're quite over the hill yet." He definitely looked good to her, a picture of athletic grace in her book. "Maybe you didn't get enough sleep last night."

His lips twitched and the corners of his eyes crinkled. "And who's fault was that?"

"You were the one doing most of the kissin'," she pointed out with a sassy lift of her chin.

Michael gave her a teasing squeeze that made her gasp with laughter. In spite of their exhausting night of making love, he still wanted to kiss her as much as he had from the first. And do a lot more than that, too, he admitted, silencing a groan that threatened.

"Come on," he said. "I want to show you a place I found when we were out catching those partridges."

"A very secluded spot, I hope."

"Very."

Once they were away from the village, fern and pine needles crunched beneath their booted feet as they walked side by side. Michael had never been so aware of the ancient voices of the forest. The murmur of fir and hemlock caressed his ears, much in the way Cassie had stroked her hands across him during the night. The whirring of wings in the treetops was as featherlight as her kisses. A stream sighed somewhere nearby, a whisper that echoed her soft sounds of pleasure.

He didn't want all of the experience to be an illusion, but his mind wouldn't let go of the painful memories. Only when he held Cassie, loved her as mindlessly as he had during the night, could he entirely forget his quilt. And then only briefly. Fear that her precious Way Quah would vanish in a shattering moment of truth gnawed in his gut.

Yellow water lilies dotted the shallow end of the pond Michael led Cassie to. Surrounding most of the shoreline were bushes covered with white blossoms, while the opening at the opposite end boasted a series of small waterfalls, where a narrow stream of water slid over slick, moss-covered rocks. Flowers resembling orchids dipped their purple petals in response to the slightest movement of air.

"Oh," Cassie said on a sigh. "It's so beautiful. So lush it's almost like Hawaii. This must truly be an enchanted place."

"I wouldn't know about that. The water's a little colder than the islands, I imagine, but still warm enough for skinny-dipping. It doesn't seem possible in this part of the country, but I think there must be an underwater thermal spring.''

Her eyes widened and her cheeks pinked. "Really?''

"Are you game?''

How could she resist? Swimming here with Michael would be a memory she could pull out of her pocket whenever she needed to feel close to him. Her Aunt Myrtle had always said a person needed some secret place to escape to when reality got a little too tough to take. This pond would be her own private haven, and she would make the memories sweet.

Setting her camera aside on a rock, she undressed quickly.

Thermal spring or not, the water temperature was cool enough to bring a gasp to her lips when it first caressed her bared flesh. She eased into the water slowly, adjusting to the lap of wavelets at the sensitive spot at the back of her knees, then across her thighs and finally at her midriff.

More courageous, Michael arrowed his way across the pool without any hesitation, a dark, sleek form of power and grace. He turned and rose up from the water like a god from the sea. His bronzed body glistened with moisture. He dived again, coming toward Cassie, and she had only a moment to react to the devilish glint in his eye before she felt his hand close around her ankle.

"No!" she cried. But it was too late. Pulled off-balance, she slid under the surface of the water, and in the crystal-clear depths she could see Michael's wicked grin.

She shoved off the bottom of the pool. Kicking her way to the surface, she burst out of the water, gasped for air and shouted a laughing threat. "I'm going to get you for that, Michael Longlake." She sent a two-handed wave of water toward him.

He wasted no time accepting her challenge for a water fight. Within minutes, she was weak with helpless laughter. She'd never seen Michael like this, full of teasing fun as he chased her from one end of the pool to the other. Not that she had a prayer of getting away from him if he decided otherwise. And she rarely got off a salvo splash in retaliation.

Collapsing on a half-submerged rock beside the waterfall, Cassie sank into the pool until the water covered the tops of her breasts. Breathlessly, she surrendered. "Enough. You win. I'm at your mercy."

"I'm glad you realize that." He found a comfortable spot to sit next to her. "You're finally beginning to understand who's boss."

"You're just bigger than me. It's not fair."

"Yeah. I know." Grinning, he dipped his head to give her a kiss, warm and sweet and tasting of springwater.

For a time they sat in silence, listening to the sounds of the forest, the songbirds calling and the breeze caressing the tops of the fir trees as softly as the water flowed over the rocks. Michael leaned back and closed his eyes.

Observing him, Cassie realized she wanted to know everything about Michael . . . what he ate for breakfast at home, his favorite movies, if he followed the foibles of the Minnesota Twins on the radio. But the first answer she needed meant she had to ask the hardest question of all.

"Michael?" she began tentatively.

"What?" came his drowsy reply.

"If I ask you something personal, would you promise not to get upset with me?"

He opened one eye. "Go ahead."

"How did your wife die?"

Everything went still. If Cassie hadn't known better, she would have sworn the birds had stopped singing and the water had stopped flowing the instant her question had left her mouth. Suddenly she wasn't so sure Running Deer had been right. Maybe she should have left well enough alone.

"You don't want to know, Cassie."

She did, and she didn't. She only wanted to know Michael as intimately as possible, and help him get past his grief if she could. But maybe this wasn't the right time. "You don't have to tell me if you don't want to."

The forest hung on the razor edge of silence waiting for Michael's response.

Slowly his husky voice found the words. "It was the end of January. Monica hadn't wanted to winter-over that year. She hated the cold and said it was too lonely on the Gunflint Trail. She thought our little boy needed playmates. We'd had some battles ... big ones." He speared his fingers through his damp hair, remembering those terrible scenes, domestic quarrels that shook the house and made Peter cry. That morning Monica had been so angry she'd thrown a plate at Michael, and still he hadn't given in. If only...

"I took them out dog sledding that afternoon," he continued. "I ran a team of eight dogs. Mixed-breed huskies, like the dogs here in the village. They needed the exercise. I thought I'd at least get Monica out of the house for a while. Break the routine. Perk up her spirits." Beneath the water his fingers flexed and clenched. "They do logging along the Gunflint Trail and trucks come and go all year. Eighteen-wheelers. At one point the dogsled trail crosses the road. I didn't hear..."

"Oh, my God. The truck hit . . ."

When Michael looked at Cassie there were tears in his eyes. "She'd made me study to be a paramedic in case anything happened to her or Peter. I sweated blood memorizing for the tests. And then when it happened, when she needed me, they both needed me . . . I couldn't do a damn thing. And it was *my* negligence that killed them . . . killed them both."

Cassie took him in her arms because she simply didn't know what else to do. He'd accepted the blame for something that wasn't his fault. He needed absolution, but it wasn't hers to give. Only Michael could forgive himself. Only he could rediscover his own happiness.

A brisk wind blew down over the trees, chilling the air and riffling the water. Wispy clouds blocked the sun. Cassie shivered when she felt unbearable pain rack Michael's strong body. She ached for him. He seemed to be slipping away from her, more in an emotional sense than in a physical way. Desperately, she held on.

"Shh, Michael. It's all right."

"No." Harsh refusal cut the word sharply. He tore himself away, wrenching free of her embrace, and stood. "I've got to go. I can't stay here." Fear and grief haunted eyes that only minutes ago had teased her with a dark glint of sexual awareness. She never should have asked her question; never should have made him remember; never should have asked him to expose his vulnerabilities.

"We'll go back to the village, if that's what you want," she offered.

His long, muscular strides took him across the pond as though there was no water there at all. The air grew cooler and the clouds thickened to blackness. Cassie hurried to cross the pool after him, wading laboriously through the waist-high water. "Wait a minute," she pleaded. "Wait for me."

"I can't, Cassie. It wouldn't do any good." He pulled up his jeans, then tugged on his shirt. "I can't give you what you want."

"I'm not asking for anything." Granted, she *wanted* a whole lot, *hoped* for a whole lot, but she had too much pride to *ask*.

Picking up his bush hat, he placed it squarely on his head, then held her gaze for three long, echoing heartbeats. "God, Cassie, I'm sorry." He turned and vanished into a gathering mist that hid the silent forest and instantly erased the sound of his footsteps. The only thing she could still sense was his pain.

The sensation tortured a tender place beneath her breastbone. "Michael?"

Cassie had never been more alone. In this strange, unfamiliar place, she shivered and shook with the deepening cold as she quickly dressed. Following

Michael, she took the path into the gray misty forest only to discover Running Deer waiting for her.

"Have you seen Michael?" Cassie asked. "He got upset when I started making him remember—"

"He is gone."

"Gone? But he was just here a minute ago. We were swimming and having fun and then—"

"He stopped believing. For a little while you helped him to find happiness, but now he has returned to that dark place which is so full of pain for him."

"But you told me if he talked about his wife his wound would heal," Cassie protested, fear clutching in her chest. "I wouldn't have said one word, not a single word, if I'd known what it would do to him."

"For some men, letting go of the past is hard."

A wave of nausea born of fear threatened. "How can I help him, Running Deer? I still feel his pain... right here...." She placed her palm on her chest as though she could ease Michael's anguish where it still echoed inside her. "Even when I can't see him I know what he's feeling." And it would always be that way, she realized. No matter what happened in her future.

"For now he is lost in that dark place and he will not be able to find his way out."

"But he's a guide. A good one."

"It was *you* who led him here. Now the only way you can release him from the place of eternal torment where he is trapped is to forgo your belief in Way Quah."

Cassie looked at the young Indian woman incredulously, her thoughts suspended between horror and fear. "How can I stop believing in Way Quah? I'm here, aren't I? I'm talkin' to you, and I've been to the village. After all Michael and I went through to get here, I can't just say you don't exist." It was real! She'd known it from the start.

Wind swirled the mist around Running Deer, fluttering the fringed hem of her deerskin skirt, and the long strands of her dark hair shifted across her shoulders. "Perhaps, in time, he will be given another chance."

"It's not just me, you know." Cassie clung desperately to her dreams. "There's folks who are counting on me. Jack and Flossie and Eldyne. And all the others. I promised 'em I'd bring back the secret of happiness and I haven't even learned it for myself yet. They believed in me." Her throat tightened as the reality of the decision she would have to make bore down on her. "My Aunt Myrtle believed, too. I can't..."

"You are a strong woman, Cassandra Seeger."

She didn't feel strong. She felt weak and wobbly and confused. Way Quah had to be real, yet now she was being asked to give up the very dream that had kept her going all those years when she had struggled to care for her aunt. They'd talked and laughed and made crazy plans for the time when they'd visit Way Quah together, knowing that part of the dream would never come true. But somehow that had made Cassie's life bearable. Now she felt a great hollowness filling her chest where once there had been hope, darkness replacing light.

For Michael, for the man she loved, she had to give up her dream. She had to convince herself there was no Way Quah. There never had been. Everything she had ever read, had ever believed in, was only a figment of her fertile imagination.

The thought paralyzed her.

"I can't," she whispered.

"I understand much is being asked of you."

She pressed her trembling lips together. How could she choose? "What about his memories of me? Will he forget everything good along with the bad stuff?"

"He never truly trusted the memories of his first journey. He will believe he imagined this new experience."

Everything? The way he'd held her, *loved* her? "Will I forget, too?" Will my pain go away?

Running Deer smiled in sad understanding and slid her hand across her distended belly. "There are some things a woman never forgets."

Cassie would remember. Every moment, every nuance, every sweet, tantalizing memory of Michael and being in his arms.

But she could not leave him in whatever purgatory had torn him away from her. Not if she had the power to bring him some small measure of peace. And without Michael in her dreams, she realized, her happiness was as elusive as he'd always said it would be.

"What do I do?" she asked in a voice as leaden as the gray mist that hovered all around her.

"Call him," Running Deer said simply. "Tell him you were wrong."

Wrong. Oh, God...

Steeling herself, Cassie suppressed every image of Way Quah, tucking the memories into that place where she had learned to put her foolish dreams away when it was time to wake up.

She peered through the heavy mist. Not a tree was visible, nor was there a sound of birds in the forest, or squirrels gathering pine nuts for the winter. Even the air carried no trace of wood smoke from the village fires, or the fragrance of flowers growing wild.

Tears she refused to shed pressed at the back of Cassie's eyes. Her dream was gone. "He'll hear me?"

When there was no answer, she blinked away the moisture and discovered she was all alone. Terribly alone.

"Michael?" she called. "Come back. Please. There isn't..." Her voice hitched. "There isn't any Way Quah. I made a mistake."

Chapter Twelve

"Stay put, Cassie. I'm coming."

Michael shouldered his way through the tight maze of pine branches in search of her. Spiky needles whipped across his face; tree limbs blocked his path. As soon as he and Cassie had stepped into the woods, leaving the canoe on the beach, Michael had lost track of both direction and time in the damp, green confusion of the forest. One minute Cassie had been there, holding his hand, dragging him through the woods. Then he'd tripped. An instant later she'd disappeared.

Vanished! As if a yawning pit had opened up in the ground and swallowed her into a dark hole. He had no idea how long she'd been gone.

Thank God he'd found her. Or maybe she had found him. Whatever the case, he felt a surge of grateful relief, as though a great weight had been lifted from his shoulders. It wasn't like him to lose his way so easily, or to misplace a client he was guiding. Particularly not one who was such a ball of stubborn vitality she made him ache for her.

Shifting his shoulders and ducking his head, he forced himself through the pine growth. In this part of the forest there was hardly enough room for a squirrel to maneuver, much less a full-grown man.

He broke out into the clearing where Cassie stood, and air lodged painfully in his lungs. She looked small and incredibly vulnerable standing alone among the pines. In a flash, his mind replayed the image of her body beneath his, Cassie making soft little sounds of pleasure as he thrust the hard length of his manhood into her hot, velvet sheath. He saw her eyes dark with passion; felt the scoring of her nails across his back, ached with a memory of what he had done.

His body reacted to the vision with the same quick, fiery intensity as it had last night in the old woman's cabin. An experience he wanted to repeat as soon as possible. Here on the pine-covered ground, if need be.

But he wasn't going to do that. Driven by wild, primitive forces he didn't understand, he'd taken advantage of Cassie. She deserved more than a quick coupling with a guy who'd slipped out of control. With bitter insight, he realized she deserved things he wasn't prepared to give, like commitment and a guarantee of happiness.

Stifling a low groan of frustration, he shook the erotic vision from his mind. He had to get this wild-goose chase in search of Way Quah over with, get back to the nice quiet life he'd led before a whirl-wind named Cassie Seeger had blown in his door. And sneaked under his skin, he mentally amended with a sharp stab of honesty, and into his dreams as well. Even now it was hard to believe he would never, ever be able to claim this woman in every hotly inti-mate way possible.

His boot snapped a twig on the ground and she whirled to look in his direction.

"Michael? Are you..." Her voice hitched uncer-tainly. "I thought I'd lost you."

He caught a sad, hopeless look in her eyes that hadn't been there before, and her mobile lips shifted downward with the press of her dismay. Somehow he had hoped to protect her from this disappointment, from the sense of betrayal that false dreams bring. As he had with his wife and son, he'd failed once again. The knowledge twisted like a hot blade in his gut.

Approaching slowly, he caught her chin with the crook of his finger and lifted, savoring the softness of her flesh, the inviting shape of her lips, the in-triguing blue of her eyes.

Filled with compassion for the disillusionment she now faced, he said, "You finally figured it out, didn't you, Cassie? There's nothing at that little white spot on your map except trees and more trees. Just like I said."

Her chin trembled before she echoed, "Just like you said."

Softly knuckling her cheek with the back of his hand, he figured it was just as well he was with Cassie when she discovered the truth. It hurt too much to face reality alone. "Heck of a trip though, wasn't it?"

"Wouldn't have missed it for the world."

He canted her a grin. "Maybe you'll come back up this way again? Do some more fishing?"

"I ... I don't know."

He wished she would ... and knew he didn't have any right to hope she'd return. He was going to miss her nonstop chatter, her bright smile that had briefly managed to lift the shadows from the dark corners of his mind. But she had her own life to lead. And he knew, never again could he condemn a woman to live in this remote area where his Indian soul resided, but where help was a fatal distance away when needed. Or where his negligence could mean the death of someone he loved.

"Let's see if we can find the canoe," he said past the unexpected thickening in his throat. "We didn't come far from the beach."

She glanced over her shoulder into the misty woods and sighed a tremulous sound. "No, not far." There was nothing visible behind her except ambiguous shadows; in the same way, Cassie saw nothing in her future except an aura of emptiness. A black void. Where had all of her hopes and dreams gone? Absorbed by the mist, she imagined. The realization caused a deep, twisting sensation low in her body.

Her attention slid back to Michael, her gaze taking in the enticing view of his bronzed skin at the vee of his shirt, perusing the strong line of his jaw and finally settling on the sculpted shape of his lips. Kissable lips. Lips that had brought her such staggering pleasure she felt deprived now by their absence on hers.

"Cassie, about last night..."

Her gaze snapped up to meet his. There was so much regret in his voice he was almost hemorrhaging remorse. "Don't say it, Michael. Please don't. No promises offered, no promises made. By either of us."

UNBELIEVABLY, AS THOUGH they'd been traveling in circles, it took less than a day to get back to Gunflint Lake.

To Michael's dismay, his grandfather started on his damn tom-tom within hours of his return.

"What is wrong now?" he demanded to know.

From the place where he sat cross-legged with his back against a tree, Snow Cloud squinted up at Michael...but he didn't miss a beat on the drum. "You have hurt that woman."

"Cassie? That's absurd." Michael's gruff retort covered a turbulent range of emotions he didn't want to face. She'd left in her rusty old car with hardly a backward glance. He figured she'd be okay once she managed to forget all about Way Quah. And him.

He wondered how long it would take him to forget about Cassie.

"I saw it in her eyes," Snow Cloud insisted. "You took the hope from her."

"I didn't do any such thing. She's just upset we didn't find a village that wasn't there in the first place."

The tom-tom stopped, only its echo still beating inside Michael's skull.

"You were both there, son of my son," Snow Cloud said in the same insistent rhythm. "Together, you reached Way Quah."

Michael had a quick vision of an Indian village...so like the one he'd seen in his youthful quest...and then a blond woman with a sassy, turned-up nose and a mouth made for kissing was running with him toward wigwams that formed a perfect square. He blinked and the image was gone.

"No, I didn't, Grandfather. Your enchanted village doesn't exist. Neither does Way Quah's promise of happiness. Cassie knows that now."

Awkwardly, Snow Cloud stood, and Michael caught his grandfather's elbow until the old man could steady himself with his walking stick.

"She gave up everything she believed in to save you, foolish grandson. Now you have nothing. Nothing at all. And she is adrift without the direction she once had."

"I can't do anything about that. She'll manage—"

Snow Cloud poked him in the chest with his walking stick. "When your wife and child died it was an accident, yet you took the blame. Now you lose a second chance for happiness and you deny you are at fault. Your eyes may see but your mind is blinded by guilt. Let the past go, Michael Longlake, or the Old Man of the Forest will have won."

Michael sucked in a painful breath. Could his grandfather know the details of the journey? Or was he simply repeating parts of the old legend?

"This time," Snow Cloud continued, his voice lowering in warning, "you ran from your fears when you should have stood and fought them."

How could he fight what he couldn't see or grasp? Michael wondered over the next few days. At odd moments while he worked, in his mind's eye he'd catch a glimpse of an Indian village, or a secluded pool with a stair-step waterfall, a wigwam and a bed of pelts. Always Cassie would be there. Smiling. Desirable. Passionate. So real he ached for her.

As he walked alone through the woods at night, he longed for her whirlwind spirit beside him. Like a man suffering through a long fast, he craved the way her presence made the stars brighter and the moon glow with more intensity.

He jammed his fingers through his hair. She was driving him crazy. She had from the start. At some very instinctive level he finally admitted the sound of his grandfather's accusing words would haunt him until he faced his own personal demons. And won.

That night he slid his canoe into the dark water on the silvery path of the moon. Cold, still air carrying the promise of approaching winter bit into his flesh. Once again he would seek Way Quah, and this time he would not turn his back on happiness.

WITH A HEAVY HEART, Cassie braced herself for her first day back at work. She hadn't found the secret of happiness she'd touted with so much confidence to the regulars at the coffee shop. Failed them, she realized. And her Aunt Myrtle, too.

She tucked the packet of pictures she'd had developed into the pocket of her blue gingham apron. The snapshots from the last roll weren't there. She hadn't had the nerve to take that final roll of film to the one-hour photo store for fear of what it might, or might not, reveal. On the drive home to the Twin Cities she'd had flashes of vague images... of Indian villages and Michael making love to her in a wigwam... that had seemed so substantial she didn't want to acknowledge they were only wishful thinking.

For the few remaining days of her vacation, she'd hibernated in her apartment, struggling to come to grips with a potpourri of emotions as wildly vacillating as a roller-coaster ride, or a trip down a chute of raging white water. Now it was time to get on with her life.

As she measured coffee for the first morning pot, she marveled at how little the café had changed in her absence, while in the same short period of time she had undergone a life-altering experience. She'd fallen hopelessly in love.

With new insight, she realized the cheery wall mural that Arletta adored looked flat and lifeless; the aging Formica countertops appeared tatty and worn. What had once lifted Cassie's spirits now pressed down on her with the unforgiving weight of futility. Perhaps she would own this coffee shop one day, but in her heart she would always know true happiness had slipped through her fingers.

The front door opened admitting a gust of cool air to mix momentarily with the warm scent of freshly brewed coffee.

"Welcome back," Flossie called cheerfully. Dressed in her usual man's work pants and wrapped in an old gray sweater, she marched across the coffee shop to the counter. Both her smile and the fact that Jack, the Vietnam vet, was right behind her were a surprise.

"Hi, yourself," Cassie responded as she poured coffee into two mugs for them.

"Caught us a big string of pike this mornin'," Flossie announced, seating herself on a swivel stool. "We're gonna have 'em for supper."

"Really?" Cassie's gaze slid from Flossie to Jack. He crooked her a little grin, the first time she'd ever seen him smile, his facial muscles moving slowly as though they were rusty.

"Yep. Jack here told me I had my lines rigged wrong all these years, then he showed me how t' cast out in them tules without gettin' snagged. Worked real good, it did." She dumped a couple of teaspoons of sugar into her cup and stirred vigorously. "Real good."

"You two were fishing together?"

"While you were gone," Jack explained in his softly spoken way, "Flossie had some trouble with her water heater. I offered to help her install a new one."

"Well now..." Cassie returned his smile. "That was nice of you, Jack." More than that, it was a decided breakthrough for two people who deserved happiness.

His narrow shoulders lifted his old leather jacket in a shrug. He was freshly shaved and for once his eyes didn't look haunted.

"Then him 'n' me got to talkin'," Flossie went on. "Did you know he won the Junior Fishing Derby right here at Lake Minnetonka in...what year was that, Jack?"

"Sixty-five, I think."

"'Course he was just a kid then, but later he went off to war and didn't get no chance to fish like he wanted. And I figured..." A blush tinged the aging hollows of her cheeks as though she was embarrassed to have done something nice for someone else.

"I'm trading handyman chores around her place for room and board."

"My own son's way off in California, and he don't have no time to mess with an old lady when he's got his own family and such. It's a big house, and the fishin's right there."

An invisible smile of pleasure fluttered Cassie's midsection. "I think that's just perfect. For both of you."

She took their orders . . . a cheese omelete and bacon for Jack, French toast for Flossie, then Flossie said, "So tell us about your trip. You find that ol' secret of happiness you was lookin' for?"

"Sure did." She forced a bright tone to cover her lie. "But it looks to me like you two don't need any help from me. I'll just save that little secret for somebody who needs it more."

"Fine with us," Jack agreed. "For myself, I figure this winter is going to be a whole lot better than last."

In a motherly gesture, Flossie patted his hand. "You ever done any ice fishin'?"

"Sure."

"Seems t' me there's an ol' ice hut stashed somewheres in the garage. It's probably broke, but I reckon we could take a look . . ."

Cassie left them to their plans while she placed their order tickets on the carousel for Arletta. At least Flossie and Jack wouldn't suffer because she had failed in her quest. On that bright note, she lifted her chin a bit. Things were going to be all right.

It was nearly noon, and Cassie's feet and her lower back were already beginning to ache, when Eldyne and Ernie showed up together for brunch. Cassie raised a curious eyebrow as she carried two mugs and the pot of decaf to the booth that had always been Ernie's private domain. More changes had gone on around Arletta's place than she had at first perceived.

"Hello, little lady," Ernie said with a wave of his hand. He looked particularly spiffy in his navy blue blazer and white turtleneck sweater. "I see you made it back safely from your grand adventure."

"Oh, yes." Her heart caught at the sight of his soft brown eyes, and she remembered all the soulful looks his namesake had given her. And how the mink had bitten Michael just before he'd almost kissed—

She forced the memory away. "Back safe and sound." With only a broken heart and a few scabby mosquito bites to show for her efforts.

"Did you bring us back some pictures, honey?" Eldyne asked.

"Dozens. It was sure pretty country." Cassie retrieved the photos from her pocket and placed them on the table. "I've got your camera in the back room. I'll bring it out as soon as I get a minute."

"No hurry." Eldyne began shifting through the snapshots. "Oh, look at this, Ernie, honey. Look at these wildflowers," she crooned. "So lovely."

"No prettier than those in your garden, my sweet little pumpkin."

Eldyne blushed and Cassie nearly dropped the coffeepot. Struggling to suppress a smile, she said, "You two seem to have gotten better acquainted while I was gone."

"Young lady, I owe you a great deal of thanks."

"You do?" She glanced at Ernie.

"All your talk about seeking the secret of happiness started me thinking. And what I decided was that I wasn't too old to have a pretty lady on my arm, so I invited Eldyne to the Chrysanthemum Festival."

"We had a lovely time." Eldyne smiled shyly across the table.

"And I intend to invite her to the potluck next week . . . and I'll bring my very own specialty, the cheesiest lasagna you've ever—"

"You'll do no such thing, Ernest Talbert Schmidt." Eldyne waggled her finger at him. "That has way too much cholesterol for you. *I'll* make up some nice broiled chicken with a—"

"Now, Ellie—"

"Don't you 'now Ellie' me. I intend for you to stay healthy for a good long time. Now that we've found each other. . . ."

Cassie headed for the back of the shop to get Eldyne's camera. It looked as if her regulars had managed far better on their own than she had. At least she hadn't disappointed them. She wouldn't want to have been burdened with that kind of guilt.

Blowing out a sigh, she shoved through the swinging door to the kitchen.

"You look a little frazzled." With the back of her hand, Arletta swept a strand of drooping gray hair away from her face. Hard work and too many samples of her own cooking had plumped up her already stocky frame.

"I guess I'm out of practice being on my feet," Cassie conceded, knowing more than a simple backache was bothering her. "At least it's cooler out front than it is back here."

"You've always had a knack of looking on the bright side." Arletta deftly flipped a grilled cheese sandwich, then pressed two burger patties onto the hot griddle. Steam lifted the aroma of sizzling beef toward the overhead vent. "Guess that's why your customers are so loyal."

"I suppose." Without paying much attention to Arletta, Cassie cranked the last roll of film the rest of the way through the camera, dropped it into its container and put it in her pocket. She'd been told in no uncertain terms there was no Way Quah and she had to let go of that dream. *No universal secret of happiness.* She was as much on her own as her regulars were.

The thought stuck in her throat as though she'd swallowed a hard-boiled egg whole.

"I'm sure they'll be just as faithful when the new owners take over."

Cassie's head snapped up. "New owners?"

"Didn't I tell you?" Arletta slid the grilled sandwich onto a plate and added a serving of french fries. "Shoot, I guess we got so busy this morning, I plumb forgot." The plate went up onto the serving counter in a spot right under the heating lamp. "My dream has finally come true. A big chain is buying me out. Paying megabucks for this location, too. Could of told 'em years ago this spot was the best site on this side of the county."

A wave of nausea threatened to overcome Cassie, so powerful and unexpected it forced her to sit down on a nearby stool. "I thought..."

"Biggest chain in the Midwest. Guess they know what they're doing. Gonna remodel the whole place."

In sterile pink-and-turquoise colors that were the chain's trademark, Cassie suspected. Modern sterile decor with no history, no love involved, no personality, no distinction from one franchise to another. "I'd always planned..."

"I made 'em promise to give my employees first crack at the new jobs. Got it in writing, too. I figured you all could use the benefits, like medical insurance, dental and such, that I've never been able to give you.''

Having her teeth cleaned at somebody else's expense seemed like a poor trade-off to Cassie for losing the last of her dreams.

''Figured you might want to apply for the manager's job. You'd be a natural.''

Nothing at the moment seemed in the least *natural*. She might end up working at Arletta's café...or for the new owners...for the rest of her life. But it would never be *hers*.

Dammit all—she deserved more than that!

She ought to...she was going to...

Like someone had slid a rod of steel right down the center of her spine, Cassie straightened. By heavens, she was going to talk to that lady at Lakeside Lodge. She was going to own that place if she had to beg and borrow from every bank in the state, or friend she'd ever known. If it took her years to pay every dime off and make it hers, she wouldn't mind.

Her fingers balled into determined fists. Lakeside Lodge was going to be hers. She could feel her new resolve tighten in her belly with the confidence of solid conviction. She didn't need Michael Longlake to make her happy any more than Eldyne or Flossie or any of the regulars needed her to tell 'em what to do. She could damn well do it on her own.

"Hello back there." Cassie turned to see Eldyne peering into the kitchen from the opposite side of the serving opening, her eyes just barely topping the waiting grilled cheese sandwich on the high counter. "Cassie, are you around?" She held one of the snapshots in her hand.

Even from across the room Cassie could tell it was a picture of Michael with his half smile canted toward the camera. "I'm here."

"Unless I miss my guess," Eldyne said, "the tall, dark hunk in this picture was your guide. Right?"

Cassie swallowed hard. A guide in more ways than she would care to admit. "That's right."

"Well then, honey, I think you ought to come out here. You've got a customer over by the cash register who looks like he's up a creek without his paddle."

Her jaw went slack at the same time her heart kicked up a beat. Michael? Here? It didn't seem possible....

Afraid to get her hopes up too high, Cassie pushed out through the swinging doors. Her palms were wet, her breathing labored. She struggled to contain the wild and wonderful sensations that coursed through her at the sight of Michael standing next to the cash register. Dressed in his camouflage shirt and jeans, he was taller than she remembered, far more broad of shoulder. When his onyx gaze touched her in a warm velvet sweep, she knew she was a goner. Again.

After a lifetime of chatter, every word she'd ever learned fled Cassie's mind. "Hi," she finally managed to say.

His tongue moistened his lips as though they were as dry as Cassie's throat. "So this is Arletta's?"

"Yeah."

"Nice."

"You want coffee? A sandwich?"

"Maybe later."

"Sure."

His eyes darted around the coffee shop to check out the lunchtime crowd. "I brought you something."

Dear God, she hoped it was a cure for her wildly flip-flopping stomach. "Maybe I should ask Arletta if she can handle the front for a minute."

"That might be best."

Cassie escaped to the kitchen, got things sorted out, then led Michael out to the back of the shop where the employees parked. In spite of the nip in the air, the sky was a crystalline blue.

"So how have you been?" she asked brightly, feeling a little more in control of her emotions after the first shock of seeing Michael had worn off. Had it only been days since she'd last seen him? Or an eternity?

"Lonely."

She had to swallow twice before she could speak. "Me, too." Even then her words were little more than a painful whisper.

He extended his hand, palm up. Resting in the center of his hand was a carefully crafted medallion created of buckskin in a delicate spidery web. Feathers and beads decorated the design.

Cassie drew in a quick breath and the forbidden vision of Way Quah came to her.

"Running Deer sent it." Michael carefully placed the gift in Cassie's hand. "She wishes you only happy dreams."

The world shifted and reshaped itself at a dizzying speed. "How...I thought...you told me..." A thousand disjointed thoughts raced through Cassie's mind along with the image of an Indian village, the scent of a wigwam made of cedar, and the erotic feel of Michael's hands caressing her, of their bodies joined.

"I went back, Cassie. I had to do it on my own."

Her forehead knitted into a tight frown. "Back?"

"To Way Quah."

She shook her head, forcing herself to suppress the images that flooded her mind, like she'd shrug off a haunting dream the morning after. "You told me it wasn't real. That's what you always said. No more than an illusion."

He lifted the medallion and tied the buckskin thongs around the back of her neck, his fingers lingering to play gently through the short hairs at her nape. "Is what you're feeling now an illusion? Am I only smoke?"

Oh, no, he was far more substantial. He was flesh and bones, a masculine scent of cedar and pine. He was love and joy and happiness. He was the man of her dreams.

Emotion thickened her words. "You're real. But how... Why?" She hesitated, afraid if she stretched the thin fabric of reality too far it would break.

"I couldn't stand not having you around. I missed your smile so much it was driving me crazy... along with Grandfather's tom-tom," he admitted. "But I couldn't let go of the past."

"There's no rule that says you have to forget your wife and son. You loved them."

"I had to forgive myself for the accident. Running Deer helped me do that."

"She did?"

He lifted the medallion and shifted it from side to side, studying the decorations carefully. "In a way, Running Deer reminded me of my mother. I can remember at night when Mother put me to bed how she always wished me sweet dreams. After she died..."

Love and respect choking her voice, Cassie said, "Maybe now you'll rest easier." She wrapped her arms around his waist and leaned her head against his chest. "Was it a hard trip back?"

"No. Not this time," he admitted, rubbing his cheek across the top of her head. "When I felt lost, I simply closed my eyes and let my thoughts of you guide me where I knew I needed to go."

"I'm glad."

"Will you marry me, Cassie? I figure I can build my birchbark canoes any place in the country. Here in the Twin Cities, if you want, or—"

"No."

He pulled back as if he'd been shot. "No?"

"I want something of my own, Michael Long-lake. Something I can build with my own hands, and I don't imagine I'd be real good at gluing together strips of bark. I want us to buy the Lakeside Lodge."

"That old place? It's all run-down—"

"That's why we'll be able to get it for a really good price. You can keep on building your canoes, if you want. Particularly in winter—"

"I'm not going to put you at risk living in Gun-flint. It's too dangerous. Too remote. What if—"

"Oh, nonsense. The Rassmusens have lived there happily till they're practically doddering. I'd settle for that, fella." She jabbed him in the chest.

"You would?"

"For the chance to hang around with the best guide in all of the boundary waters? The man I just happen to love? You're darn right I would."

His smile started slowly, twitching the corners of his mouth until the grin could no longer be contained. It broke across his face like sunrise greets the day. "Cassie Seeger, you are the most incredible woman I have ever met."

"You got that right, big guy."

A flush tinged his cheeks. "I love you."

She blew out a sigh. "I sure was hoping for that." And maybe in her heart of hearts, she'd never quite given up her dream.

He pulled her into his arms and held her hard against his chest for a hundred heartbeats.

"So how did your pictures turn out?" he finally asked.

"Real good. Most of them." Particularly the one of Michael, which she planned to have blown up to eight-by-ten, and the sweet little picture of Ernie staring up at her with those big brown eyes.

"Most?"

"Well, I...I didn't have the last roll developed. It was all of Way Quah, or so I thought, and I didn't quite know what it would show. If anything." At some level she'd probably clung to the faintest hope that her dreams had been true...and now Michael had confirmed her quest for Way Quah had been successful.

"Oh, yeah? Where's the film?"

She pulled the canister from the pocket of her apron. "What should I do with it?"

"Let me." He opened the can, removed the roll and tugged the film to its full length until he had exposed every single frame.

"What are you doing?" she complained as the last of her fantasies drifted away. "Those pictures could have proved Way Quah is real."

"Don't you see, Cassie? If you love me, and I love you, then whether or not an enchanted village exists doesn't make any difference. We can go back there any time we want."

She stared at him as though he'd lost his mind. "It took us days to find the place. We had to climb up a vertical cliff, survive the wildest rapids *you'd* ever seen, then we fought off a bear—"

"Let me show you, Cassie," he demanded in a sultry voice, lowering his head to cover her mouth with a kiss.

The moment their lips touched, Cassie was lost, lost in a dreamworld of sensuous feeling, a mystical place that floated somewhere between reality and heaven. She wasn't going to argue. All of her awareness was centered on the warm, moist feel of Michael's lips, the way his tongue partnered with hers, and how he cupped her buttocks and pulled her against the rigid feel of his arousal. Nothing else mattered. Only vaguely was she aware of the sweet scent of pinewood burning in an open fire pit, the smell of cedar all around her and the soft pillow of furs on her back.

For the rest—to protect her from bad dreams—she'd simply trust her medallion ... and holding Michael in her arms for the rest of her life.

Epilogue

"Tell us the story, Daddy. Tell us about the Dream Catchers."

Outside Lakeside Lodge, wind whipped snow across the frozen expanse of the lake, piling up drifts by the shore. The arctic cold snapped tree branches with a sound as sharp as gunfire. Inside, the crackling logs in a huge rock fireplace poured warmth into the room where the family gathered.

Michael beat a soft cadence on his grandfather's tom-tom. "You know that story as well as I do," he complained to his dark-eyed eight-year-old son, who lay sprawled on the hooked rug in front of the hearth.

"Please, Daddy," his six-year-old daughter cajoled, her sweet smile irresistible, her expression so animated she seemed always on the verge of a laugh.

"Very well . . ." In his mind, Michael slipped back in time. "The Dream Catchers live in a place called

Way Quah. It's a magical sort of place where all the good and the bad of your past come together in one moment of time. But it is very hard to find," he warned. "To get there you must overcome many obstacles, and you must keep on believing in Way Quah all the rest of your life, no matter what happens."

"And then you will be happy," the boy said staunchly.

Michael shook his head. "Then you will know you are strong enough to survive any ordeal and have within your own power the secret of happiness."

"Will you take me there someday?" his daughter asked.

"No, sweetheart, a person must find his own way." He smiled as Cassie sat down on the arm of his chair and rested one hand on his shoulder. In his eyes she had barely aged a day since she'd arrived like a whirlwind in his shop that first time. Her hair still seemed to have captured the sunlight, making long winter days along the Gunflint Trail bright with her presence.

"And if you cannot find Way Quah on your own," he continued, sliding his arm around her waist and resting his hand on her belly swollen with their next child, "then you must find a guide to show you the way. Like I found your mother."